On the Right Side
of a Dream

On the Right Side of a Dream

A Novel

Sheila Williams

One World
Ballantine Books • New York

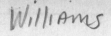
Williams

On the Right Side of a Dream is a work of fiction. Names, characters, places, and incidents are the products of the author's imagination or are used fictitiously. Any resemblance to actual events, locales, or persons, living or dead, is entirely coincidental.

A One World Books Trade Paperback Original

Copyright © 2005 by Sheila Williams
Reader's Guide copyright © 2005 by Random House, Inc.

Published in the United States by One World Books, an imprint of The Random House Publishing Group, a division of Random House, Inc., New York.

One World is a registered trademark and the One World colophon is a trademark of Random House, Inc.

Library of Congress Cataloging-in-Publication Data

Williams, Sheila (Sheila J.)
On the right side of a dream : a novel / by Sheila Williams.
p.   cm.
ISBN 0-345-46475-3
1. Bed and breakfast accommodations—Fiction.   2. Inheritance and succession—Fiction.   3. African American women—Fiction.
4. Haunted houses—Fiction.   5. Women cooks—Fiction.
6. Montana—Fiction.   I. Title.

PS3623.I5633O5 2005
813'.6—dc22   2004059566

Printed in the United States of America

www.oneworldbooks.net

2   4   6   8   9   7   5   3   1

First Edition

*This book is dedicated to
all of the "Juanitas" of the world—
don't be afraid to take the first step.*

There are years that ask questions and
there are years that answer.

—ZORA NEALE HURSTON

When you set out on your journey to
Ithaca, pray that the road is long, full of
adventure, full of knowledge . . .

—CONSTANTINE P. CAVAFY

Acknowledgments

This book was fun to write. Juanita took me on another journey of the body and spirit. I had a great time. Many thanks are due to the people who added so much to the experience.

Thank you to Dr. R. Earl Bartley for lending his medical expertise to me for a little while. Thanks, Earl! I also extend my thanks to Chefs John Kinsella, James Myatt, and Jeffrey Shelton and to the staff of the Cincinnati State Technical and Community College, Culinary Arts division. I spent the better part of a summer "in school" and have a great appreciation and respect for the hard work, tenacity, and artistry of chefs. My sincere thanks to the students of Chef Kinsella's cooking class and Chef Myatt's baking class of the summer 2003 session. Their patience, sense of humor, and dedication made my experience worthwhile. Any errors, omissions, or weird flights of fancy relating to the information provided by my "experts" are entirely my fault.

Thank you, Lori Bryant Woolridge, for lending me your support and enthusiasm. Special thanks to Lynn Hightower for your guidance and sense of humor—I appreciate it more than you know.

As always, I want to thank my family for their love and support: my sister, Claire Williams, my brother-in-law, Derrick Morrison, my wonderful children, Bethany and Kevin Smith, and my husband, Bruce Smith.

This book could not have been written without the love and encouragement of my mother, Myrtle Jones Humphrey, who passed away on April 3, 2004. While her passing has often left me without words during this past year, the light of her adventurous spirit shines through this story, and through my life.

On the Right Side
of a Dream

Chapter One

A wise woman said that there are years that ask questions and there are years that answer. For a long time, I was a sorry soul caught between the two—never going forward and afraid to look back. Wedged in between a rock and a boulder and going nowhere. That's a waste of a life and you don't get it back. But, I'm a slow learner so none of this wisdom penetrated my hard head until I was past forty. By then, the years of questions had added up. And I didn't have any answers. All I had was a beat-up suitcase, a tired-looking shoulder bag, and a few pennies. And the courage it took to listen to my own heart when it told me to take the first step, even though I was scared to death.

I ran away from home. Did not stroll, skip, or saunter. I ran as fast as I could. In my journal, I wrote that I was running away from my old life. But I was really running away from *no* life.

Now, my family was not having any of this running

away stuff. You see, they'd been so used to me being a part of *their* dramas that it never occurred to them that *I* might want a drama of my own. And not the bad kind, either.

"What's wrong with you, Juanita?" my sister asked me. "Have you lost your mind?"

My son, Randy, asked me, "Are you ever coming back?"

My kids acted as if I was leaving them to starve to death even though they were grown and living life *their* way on *my* dollar and *my* emotions. I had to fight them to get out the front door. The second-shift supervisor at the hospital where I worked could hardly keep her no-lips from curling up into a Snidely Whiplash smirk.

"Don't think you can get this position back when you run out of money," she'd told me. "In this economy, I can fill your job with the snap of a finger." When she said that, it was my turn to smirk. Exactly *when* did a nurse's aide job become a "position"?

The man in the bus station looked at me funny when I told him I was going to Montana to see what was there. He probably thought that I was an early release from a mental hospital. But the little man at the pawn shop hit the nail on the head.

"New life?" he'd asked, handing me the receipt for the suitcases I had just bought. "Where's that?"

I left to find out.

Some months later, I left Paper Moon, Montana. It was a rainy fall morning and I sat in the cab of Peaches Bradshaw's truck, crying my eyes out because I was leaving a man who loved me and folks who thought I walked on water and didn't cook too bad, either. But I wasn't running away this time. Oh, I still carried a suitcase, a tote bag, and a purse without much money in it. But for this trip, I had something else along that I hadn't had before. I had a life.

And I wore it proudly like a woman wears a big pink hat to church on Easter Sunday.

"I'll keep your side of the bed warm," Jess had told me when we'd said our good-byes in the early morning. Those were the only words I needed to hear. What can you say to a man who'll do that for you? All I could do was bury myself in his arms. If you are loved, it's enough by itself.

Millie Tilson, Paper Moon's resident eccentric, glamour girl, and innkeeper, had given me the benefit of her advice and many years of life. However many that was.

"Ohhh, I wish that I could go with you, but the Doc and I are headed to Vegas in a few weeks and we're taking tango lessons. Did I tell you that?"

"The Doc" was Millie's "boy toy," Dr. Angus Hessenauer, a seventy-something retired internist who'd grown up in Lake County, made good in Boulder, and was now back to renovate and live on the old family homestead. Their relationship (Millie said it was an "affair," *not* a relationship. "Relationships are what people have with their bankers nowadays.") was the talk of the town. No one knew exactly how old Millie *was* but everyone was in agreement that she was at least ten years older than Doc Hessenauer. Maybe more.

"Yes, you told me that," I said, watching as she unpacked a UPS box. It was her latest order from Victoria's Secret, a lacy little number in red and a few other very small pieces that could loosely be called "clothing." That's all I'm going to say about that.

"Oh, well," Millie sighed as she checked over the invoice with the focus of a C.P.A. "Be sure to go places that you've never been before. That's when you have the best adventures."

I laughed. That would be easy.

"Millie, I haven't been *anywhere* before!"

Her dark-blue eyes twinkled with mischief and wisdom.

"Then you're going to have a marvelous time, aren't you?"

I was. Everything would be new to me, every sight, every smell. But would it be "marvelous" as she said? Or, would "marvelous" have to share a space with "boring" or "sad" or "awful"?

"Sometimes, it all comes together, Juanita," Millie reminded me. "It's what you do with it. That's what matters."

She was right.

A long time ago, it seems a hundred years ago now, on the bus trip from Ohio, I'd made a list of the places that I wanted to go in my life. A wish list. Looked them up on a map, circled them with a highlighter: Los Angeles, the Yucatán, Jupiter, Tahiti, Cairo, Buenos Aires, Ursa Major, Beijing, and Auckland. I had bright orange lines crisscrossing the atlas. When I showed the list to Peaches, she laughed.

"Juanita, I don't think the Purple Passion will make it across the Pacific. Flotation is not a strong suit of the Kenworth," she'd told me, referring to her bright purple truck cab. "Beijing! Tahiti! I can see you now in a hula skirt!"

I could see me, too. It was a comical sight.

"Can't help you with Jupiter. You'll need an engine bigger than mine for that."

"Oh, that's OK," I said. Jupiter was just a silly thought that popped into my head. If you're going to make a wish list, make it good. You never know.

"Would you settle for Los Angeles? Or the Grand Canyon? And I think I might be able to manage Denver, although I don't usually pull the eastern jaunts. Stacy does those."

Stacy was Peaches's partner both professionally and personally: a tall, skinny thing with the vocabulary of a truck driver (which she was) and the heart of a poet. She got weepy over *Sonnets from the Portuguese.*

Peaches grinned. " 'Course, in a few months, I'll be heading to San Diego. How about going south into Mexico? Stacy could fly down and meet us if she doesn't have a run. I have a taste for some real tequila and a few days on the beach," Peaches commented with a sigh. I knew that thoughts of limes and frosted margarita glasses danced around inside her head.

"It's a deal," I'd agreed.

The plan was to head west through Idaho and Oregon, then south into California on I-5. Peaches had a delivery in Redding, then planned to take a detour so that I could see the ocean.

But it rained a lot that fall. And plans are meant to be changed.

"Any other time, I'd say we were lucky to have rain," Peaches yelled over the roar of the huge engine, Bonnie Raitt's deep, bluesy voice, and the swooshing sound of the windshield wipers that reminded me of the eyelashes of a giant giraffe. "It could be snow. Shoot, this is October, it *should* be snow!" she commented, squinting as she tried to see through the sheets of water that poured over the window. "This rain is not a good thing."

She was right. It got so bad that she pulled off the road a couple of times because she couldn't see. The storms rolled in from Idaho as they liked to do but instead of moving on and moving out, they brought relatives with them. The sky went dark in the late morning and stayed that way for the rest of the day so that you couldn't tell when day turned to night. Got so I expected to see Noah and his boat floating by any minute.

We got used to seeing orange cones and the flashing lights of emergency cruisers. State troopers stood in the middle of the highway directing traffic around fender benders, mud, and rock slides. It was slow going and hard on Peaches. She looked exhausted. And the three mammoth-sized cups of coffee that she'd had weren't any help.

"I hope you don't have any business appointments tomorrow morning," Peaches said, a weary smile lighting up her face.

I shrugged my shoulders.

"I'll just have my secretary reschedule," I told her. "I wish I could help you drive, though. Make this trip easier." I'd asked her once to teach me to drive the Purple Passion and she let me work through the gears. That was a chore. There's a lot to it. You can't get it in a one-hour lesson. Making turns, parking, backing up, just putting on the brakes (at seventy miles per hour) with thousands of pounds behind you took some doing.

She snorted and shook her head. She'd taken off her baseball cap and her long, sun-streaked blonde hair fell down her shoulders.

"Don't worry 'bout it. Hell, I've been driving this route by my lonesome for years. It's a treat just to have a real person to talk to. Half the time, I'm talking to myself. You know how strange *that* looks?"

The gears complained as Peaches moved through them. A trail of red brake lights wound down the highway, breaking through the soupy view of the window, flickering like Christmas-tree bulbs. The rain was getting worse. It was beyond raining cats and dogs; this was like raining cows and horses. I couldn't see a thing and didn't know how Peaches managed. The truck came to a groaning stop. Through the drippiness, a man ran down the center of the highway between the lines of stopped cars and trucks. He waved at the pickup in front of us then headed toward the Purple Passion, motioning for Peaches to roll down the window. His jacket was soaked and the rain dripped off the bill of what used to be a green John Deere baseball cap.

"What's going on?" Peaches yelled. "Accident?" Words were used with a lot of economy.

"Mud slide, road's closed," he yelled back, his eyes blinking to beat back the raindrops that were blowing in sideways. "They're going to detour to a county highway running southwest. It winds a bit but y'oughta get to the redwoods before your kid goes to college. Have to sit on it awhile, though. They're just gettin' started." He ran off to the FedEx truck in the next lane.

"I guess that's it. You will be late for that business meeting, Mrs. Louis," Peaches said, yawning, as she rolled up the window. She leaned into her seat and closed her eyes for a moment to take a catnap.

Later, when the truck began to move again, I studied the rain, the direction that the wind was blowing, and the huge rock-and-mud concoction that had spilled across the highway. I thought about the change of seasons in Montana, where summers are short and winter seems to last forever, or so they tell me. The land is so wide, so open that, even with the mountain ranges, you can see the weather coming from way off. I remember standing on the back porch of the diner with my hand to my forehead like a sentinel, watching a thunderstorm roll in across the Bitterroot and thinking to myself how beautiful it was. The skies turned from blue to milky gray, then to a silvery slate shade. A giant hand had plated the bowl of the horizon with pewter. I used to keep Jess's dog, Dracula, inside if it got too hot in August, listened to the weather on the radio just to keep up with the temperature. Sometimes, I planned out what I would cook at the diner where I worked based on the weather. If it rained and got a little cool, I put together a soup; if it was as hot as the Sahara, I whipped up cool salads and fruit. In between, I did whatever made me feel good.

I hadn't done that before I came out west, hadn't paid attention to the weather. Never even noticed it. If it rained or if it didn't, none of that ever mattered before I came to Paper Moon. When I worked at the hospital back in Columbus, I carried around a cheap fold-up umbrella (that I'd fixed with masking tape every time it blew inside out) in my tote bag, along with my lunch every day, whether it was hot or not, whether it snowed, whether it didn't.

I wasn't rooted to anything but asphalt and concrete. And buildings don't reflect the season's changes. Or a life's changes, for that matter. No way a paved parking lot tells you spring is around the corner or that it's going to rain. I am now a woman of the earth, a weather vane.

I sniff the air for rain, listen to the birds, and check the western skies for clouds. I grab a handful of dirt to feel how dry it is. I can fix the time of the sunset just by its color. And when the wind blows, I play a game with myself: Where is it coming from? How does it smell? Dust from Texas, magnolia from Alabama, corn from Indiana, pine from British Columbia.

It's hard to believe now that I lived my life in such a way

that I never noticed the rain. And I didn't notice the sun-shine much either. Barely noticed the seasons at all, as if I was immune to rain or shine. Now, that is pitiful. I shook off the memory of that poor woman, closed my eyes, and listened to the swish-swish of the windshield wipers.

Rain has two effects on me; it either makes me sleepy or makes me want to go to the bathroom. Since there weren't any rest stops in sight and running into a flash flood to pee didn't appeal to me, I took a nap. I have learned to sleep sitting up with the roar of the Purple Passion's engines as background music for my dreams. It is a funny combina-tion. In my dreams, I might be running through a meadow filled with wildflowers. But, instead of the smoky molasses smoothness of Roberta Flack's voice or the gentle sliding sounds of violins, I hear the drone of a truck's engine or the scraping sound of the shifting gears to go along with the blue skies, gold, red, and purple flowers, and gentle breezes. Oh, well. You have to make do with what you have.

I have a few ideas in my head about what I want to do next, where I want to go. A few ideas, not just one, so when folks ask me, "What you doing next, Juanita?" I sound like an idiot when I answer, "Oh, I don't know, a lot of things." Anything I haven't done, which is just about everything.

Jess and I liked to talk early in the morning, way before the birds got up. In the cool darkness, we would wrap around each other like two hands clasped in prayer and talk and argue and laugh at bad jokes until one of us would fall asleep again, usually me. And Jess would ask, "What you gonna do for an encore, Juanita? Is there a sequel to this great adventure?"

He does not ask me to give up my dreams, whatever

they turn out to be. And he doesn't make me feel guilty for wanting to wander like a gypsy, either. Just lets me know that I am always in his heart.

"You want to get married, old woman?" he'd asked once, nuzzling my neck with the tip of his nose.

Lord, no. I'd be in the running with Zsa Zsa Gabor or Elizabeth Taylor as the most married woman in America.

"I love you, *old* man," I told him, "but I'd rather live in sin if you don't mind."

My mother is rolling around in her grave. "Better to marry them and be miserable than live in sin and be happy" would have been her motto. I haven't figured that one out yet. But I am way too old now for bridal white and orange blossoms and all of the magic tricks and illusions that go with them, not that I ever went that way. No time for that. Just need a warm body next to mine. And an open heart.

Jess had laughed. The sound of his laughter, the warmth of his breath on the back of my neck had made me smile. I felt sleepy.

"Thought that I'd better ask," he'd told me, his voice softening, his words coming out slower. He yawned. "I knew you'd say no, but you'd raise hell with me if I didn't at least *ask*."

"You got that right," I had told him, closing my eyes again.

At least, I've been asked.

"Just make this your home, Juanita," he says, softly now. He takes my hand and places it on his heart, a warm place on his bare chest. "Make this your home . . ."

I see Jess's face off and on in my dreams as I fight bulls in Chihuahua, make crepes in a Toronto bistro, or climb

Mount McKinley . . . no, take that dream out, I am afraid of heights! Everywhere I go, no matter how far away it is, I see Jess's face.

"Make this your home . . ." Juanita's place.

I open my eyes. The rain has stopped but it's still drippy outside, the dampness slinking off the leaves of the trees like green gravy that hasn't thickened right. The eastern sky is a strange shade of yellow and orange, the western sky is the color of slate, a dark, angry gray with clouds of silver and black. Zigzags of lightning flicker in the distance. Peaches is playing Nina Simone now, *Sinnerman*. The clicks of the music are offbeat from the plops of rain that have started to hit the windshield. Peaches turns on the wipers again. I close my eyes.

Sometime, during my dream, Nina's voice fades and the background music that comes from the truck's engine is replaced by a loud, heavy roar. Not a groan or screech like an old car that gets stuck in first gear. And it gets loud, then it gets soft, and then it gets loud again. Over and over and over. But when the roar softens, I hear birds calling to each other and the clanging of a bell in the distance. And splashing. I am running in my bare feet through a meadow of water instead of wildflowers . . . splashing?

I woke up so fast that I jumped and almost hit my head on the visor. The truck has stopped, its engine idling. The cab was quiet and empty. No Peaches. I looked around the parklike setting and then I stared. I rubbed my eyes. I didn't believe what I saw. Peaches waved her arms to get my attention.

"Hey, Miss America!" she screamed. "I hope you got a thong bikini with you!"

I stared.

She looked like hell with her pants legs rolled above her knees. Peaches has legs like tree trunks. There was a fairly strong wind and her hair was flying every which way. She looked like a kid in a Disney World commercial.

But that's not what I was staring at.

I didn't even bother to open the door; I leaned out of the window, just looking at this thing in front of me. It roared and it crashed against the rocks. It's gray, no. It's kind of bluish-gray, no, it's green. I didn't know what color it was but it was big and loud and it went on forever.

And I have only seen it in movies.

I ran to the water's edge, kicked off my shoes and socks, rolled up my pants, and stuck my foot in. And shrieked!

The water was cold!

"It is late fall, Juanita," Peaches yelled. "Even if it is California!"

I have always wanted to see the ocean. I'd heard about it and read about it and I'd seen it on TV but nothing gets you ready for the real thing. It comes in and goes out and comes in again and the white-tipped waves and the foam look the same every time. But they aren't the same.

I put my hand up to my forehead and looked out to the end of the world, looking farther than I did when I looked east across the Montana plains toward Illinois. And I wondered now if those ancient sailors weren't right. The world is flat. The pelicans dove after fish and bobbed along the water like the apples we used to grab with our teeth from my grandmother's tin tub. The gulls screeched. I stood there with my mouth open in amazement.

"And I thought *I* was country!" Peaches teased me. "You haven't seen the ocean before?"

Why? Does it show?

"No, I haven't." I closed my eyes and took a deep breath and the salty air filled my lungs. The air smelled deep, rich, and old and I would not forget the smell as long as I live.

I wonder how the first woman felt, seeing this water for the first time. Did she stand here, with her mouth open and her eyes closed and smile as the heavy ocean breezes whipped around her face? Or did she just stare, eyes unblinking, wondering how far it went, what moved beneath the water, and if this rock that she stood on was the end of the world?

She was probably a lot more practical than I was. She probably thought about food, fishing, or building a boat.

I was just too awestruck for those kinds of thoughts.

I stood there until my toes went numb from the cold water. Just stood there in one place. I looked down at my feet and watched the water come in over my toes and then go back again. And each time I thought it might be the same water. But, of course, it wasn't.

As we drove away, it occurred to me that's what I want—for something, just one thing, to stay the same. But only good things. Could they please stay good, 'cause I've had enough ugliness in my life. I have moved away from that mess, and I want someone to tell me that the joy I've found will stay with me awhile. That I'll be able to pull it over my head and wear it like an old soft sweatshirt whenever I need it, for as long as I need it.

You know all those cities I have wanted to visit? Buenos Aires, Beijing, New York, Hong Kong? I have learned something new about myself: I don't like cities much anymore.

Peaches drove into Los Angeles from the north. Some

miles out I saw an orange-brown cloud that floated over the skyscrapers like a shawl thrown over a woman's shoulders. But this was not a delicate, soft length of cashmere that was made to keep the evening chill away. It was a rough wool blanket, scratchy and thick. In some places, the haze was murky and more brown than orange. And it wasn't lightly perfumed. It was stinky.

We were traveling through the city on I-5 and, in both directions, the traffic was bumper-to-bumper, moving slower than a constipated snail. Car horns honked, middle fingers went up every place you looked, and I saw more fists raised in the air on that highway than I had in 1969 at a Black Panther rally.

"Must be some accident," I commented. "They'd better get it cleared out soon. This is a mess."

Peaches chuckled.

"There's no accident; it's like this all the time. In LA, everybody drives. *Everybody.* The freeway looks like this all day. You might get a clear highway at 3:00 AM, which is when I usually come through here."

"Oh," was all I could think of to say. I was used to cities but not ones this spread out. Even Cleveland was not *this* big or this busy. I had seen traffic, but not like this. You couldn't pull over, you couldn't pull off. You were stuck.

But when we finally got off, somewhere in the central part of the city, I think, I saw things that I was familiar with. It didn't take me long to realize that I didn't want to be familiar with them anymore: the hustle and bustle and noise of buses, diesel fuel blowing from their exhausts and music that I didn't want to hear blasting from cars as they bounced down the avenue. The souped-up Firebirds had speakers bigger than their engines. All you heard—and felt—was the bass thumping. The yelling, the cursing, the boarded-up buildings, and piece-a-cars sitting at stop-lights. We drove down one street and I thought that I'd passed into the *Twilight Zone* of lives lived. I saw myself walking down the avenue, carrying a bag of groceries or standing back from the curb, waiting for a bus. It was as if someone had said "Welcome back, Juanita." Young boys stood around and didn't seem to be doing anything except trying to look as if *they* were the alpha *and* the omega, while they tried to keep their pants from falling down around their ankles. Do they know that they walk funny? And there was always someone looking out for the uni-formed men and their flashing lights. I had to blink to keep from seeing Rashawn on those corners, digging a huge roll of Fort Knox–backed paper out of his pocket, explaining his position in a low, soft but menacing tenor. Hundreds of miles away and in cities in between, there were street corners and alleys and vacant lots just like the ones I left behind. That didn't make me feel good.

There were people everywhere, walking fast and wear-ing sunglasses. Lots of sun, lots of noise. And not much grass and no pine trees and no lakes or rivers, and we were too far into the city to see the ocean anymore. Later, I re-membered seeing the mountains at dusk as they struggled to show me their beauty through the murky haze. I saw the "HOLLYWOOD" sign, too, from a distance. I hadn't been there but a few hours and I'd already decided that I had seen enough.

But I was wrong.

Chapter Two

"If you're going to LA," Jess had told me before I left, "then you're going to Yancey's."

I'd been packing, it was nearly 1:00 AM, and the last thing I wanted to do was argue with this man. I was having a hard enough time trying to close this stupid suitcase. I pushed the lid down. Damn. It wouldn't close again. Of course, it might have been because of the two bra straps that were sticking out on the sides.

"*Not* going," I told him. "I don't have any after-five clothes. Not unless Wal-Mart sells them."

"Move."

Jess maneuvered me out of the way, opened the lid of my suitcase, and stared.

"No wonder the damn thing won't close." He picked up the sweater that I had squished on top, then glared at me. I shrugged my shoulders. "You can't pack a suitcase for shit, you know that?" He pulled out my other clothes.

"Hey!" I moved to stop Jess. He bumped me out of the way.

"There's a right way and there's a wrong way," he bellowed back. "You . . ." he shook his head in disgust. "*You* should have been in the military."

Every time I don't do something the way Jess does it, he sneers at me and says that I should have been in the army.

"Jess Gardiner, it is 1:00 AM, I am not going to talk about whether or not I would have survived the army and you are *not* going to repack my suitcase. Close the damn thing for me, and let's go to bed."

Jess ignored me and continued packing my clothes with everything buttoned, sleeves smoothed and folded with sharp right angles. By the time he finished arranging my stuff in that tired little suitcase, I had enough room for the dog if I'd wanted to take him. We did not, however, stop arguing.

"I'll call Yancey. You and Peaches can have dinner at his restaurant while you're there. That way, you'll see a four-star restaurant, Beverly Hills-style."

Yancey was an army buddy of Jess's whose bistro was world-famous. He was always showing up on TV or in celebrity magazines and Jess even said that he'd been talking to the Food Network about doing a television show but the producers were afraid to use him because he cursed too much.

"Jess, I don't have any Beverly Hills clothing," I told him.

"If you'd listen to me, woman, you'd hear that you don't have to dress up. Yancey tells me those Hollywood types wear everything under the sun. Just throw on a pair of pants and a blouse and you'll be fine."

Just like a man. Never ask him what you should wear when you are going somewhere. He'll always tell you the same thing. "Just throw on" this or that.

But my reluctance to visit Yancey's was rooted in more than being self-conscious about clothing. My experience eating out was pretty limited. Oh, I'd managed the diner, all right. Fast-food places and greasy spoons in Montana, Idaho, and Wyoming were fine and comfortable. But fancy bistro uppity places? Just the thought made my legs shaky.

"What if I use the wrong fork?" I asked.

Jess smiled, snapped the suitcase shut, and set it in the corner.

"Juanita, you think those Hollywood folks grew up knowing a salad fork from a fish fork? Most of them prob'bly never saw a demitasse cup until they hit it big. Don't be intimidated. You're as much a high-class lady as they are."

This is a man who looks at me through rose-colored bifocals, no doubt about it.

There's a fish fork?

"OK, OK, I'll go," I agreed, just to get him to stop picking at me. "But what kind of food does he serve? Real food, or will I have to stop at McDonald's afterward?"

At that comment, Jess looked sheepish.

"Oh. Uh. Well, yeah, you might want to do that. Yancey's a great chef but he does belong to the 'less is more if it's beautifully arranged on the plate' school."

Just as long as he didn't use shitty, I mean, shitake mushrooms, I thought.

Yancey's is tucked away on a side street just off Rodeo Drive in Beverly Hills. It is a place that is 180 degrees different from Jess's diner. It has a wine cellar, a huge glass-paneled bar, and a place where folks can smoke cigars, men *and* women. You have to call a month ahead to get a table because it is a place to be seen and to see (or something like that). But, thanks to Jess, Peaches and I didn't need a reservation and we got the best table in the place.

Yancey Carl is a West Virginia boy who served with SSG Jess A. Gardiner's unit in 1966. He was pulled onto a chopper by that stone-faced sergeant after he took shots in the leg and abdomen. There isn't anything Yancey wouldn't do for Jess.

"Almost fell off my stool when I got the phone call," Yancey told us. He seated us himself, served our drinks, and now sat at the table shooting the breeze despite the frantic waving of a familiar-looking woman across the aisle who was trying to get his attention. Peaches's eyes were huge. And she was . . . pointing.

"Juanita, isn't that . . . ?"

I swatted her hand down. Sometimes, Peaches is not cool at all. It was what's-her-name from one of those TV shows that I don't watch.

"How is the old sergeant?" Yancey asked.

"Still growls a little," I told him.

Peaches looked doubtful.

"No, he growls *a lot*," she corrected me. Now Peaches was trying to sneak a peek at whoever-that-woman-was without looking like she was trying to sneak a peek. That didn't work either. Peaches is a lot of things, but subtle isn't one of them.

Yancey enjoyed hearing that.

"Yeah, he usta growl at me, too. I sure miss him. Have to get out your way someday." He looked around at the busy

restaurant now filling up with patrons. "When things settle down. If they ever do." He pointed out some items on
the menu and made a few recommendations. "Pick what
you want, it's on the house. If it weren't for the sergeant, I
wouldn't be here to cook up these fancy smantzy dishes.
My momma says I've come a long way from sausage gravy
and watercress greens. Oh! Save some room for dessert.
Wendy Stern is my pastry chef and she's A-plus."

The wine was good. (Peaches says it was "great" but she
knows a lot more wine than I do. My experience is limited
to Boone's Farm.) And the food was good, too. What there
was of it.

Jess was right. Yancey cooks from the less-is-more-
just-add-a-sprig-of-parsley-or-rosemary school. There was
a nice, round, thin ("thin" was the most important word
here) slice (only one) of rare (extremely rare, so rare that
it was scary) roast beef resting in a pool of *au jus* (I know
about "oh juices" now), along with finely chopped scal-
lions (I call 'em "green onions"), and a nice, large, *very* green
piece of parsley. Think Emerald City green. A teaspoon of
garlic mashed potatoes (What is the point of just a teaspoon of mashed potatoes? That's hardly worth the effort!). Oh, and two beautifully cut (and very thin) strips of
carrot.

I looked at my plate. Peaches looked at hers as if it was
a plate of gold, said, "Hmmm . . . maybe I should have ordered two . . . ," and dug in, using both hands. I looked
back at my plate.

From over my shoulder, I heard Yancey say, "Is something wrong, Juanita?"

I am not an herbivore. I do eat meat. I just don't want to
eat it while it's still breathing. That tiny little slice of roast

beef was so rare that its blood pressure was higher than mine. I could barely look at it.

"Um, Yancey, could I get . . . I like to have my prime rib . . . medium, if that's OK." I knew those were killer words to a chef, and I wasn't even a paying customer, but what could I say?

Yancey chuckled and whisked the plate away.

"Don't worry about it," he said, a huge grin splitting his face. "You're in good company. My momma only comes here once a year. Says she can't stand the food I serve and the crowd of fakes that I serve it to. 'Puttin' on airs' she says. *And* she makes me serve her roast beef medium, too."

I finished my dinner and gave my compliments to the chef. And then Yancey brought out the dessert tray.

You never know when lightning will strike, when a flash of inspiration will appear and push you in a new direction. Destiny crossed my path in the form of the dessert tray.

There was a pudding that looked as if it had been whipped up with clouds. A three-layer lemon cake with soft ivory-colored icing that had sparkles in it. The apple tart was big enough for four people to eat or six if you counted the gigantic scoop of homemade vanilla ice cream on the side, and then a chocolate dessert with a white chocolate pyramid on top. It was called "Chocolate Death on the Nile." They were so beautiful. Each one was like something that you could see in an art museum. They had been sculpted, designed, and measured. They had been crafted. I looked at that little pyramid every which way. Peaches was through.

"Juanita, the man has other tables to wait on. Are you going to order that cake or pray over it?"

I couldn't answer her. I had turned myself into a pretzel so that I could look at the underside of the pyramid. I ordered two desserts. Not even to eat them. I just wanted them on my plate so that I could study them up close and touch them. It was hard to believe that they were food.

OK, I did have a few bites.

As I shoveled in a forkful of the lemon cake, I asked Yancey to tell his pastry chef that she was a genius.

"Yeah, she is. But you're welcome to tell her yourself."

Wendy Stern had a wide, toothy grin and tired brown eyes set in a friendly face. Her short dark-brown hair was cut like a pixie's. She blushed when I told her how much I enjoyed her desserts—looking at them *and* eating them.

"I almost feel bad getting paid to do something that I enjoy so much," she said in a quiet voice that was hard to hear over the banging of pots and pans and the yelling in the kitchen.

"Almost," she chuckled. I could hear the flat ranch lands of Texas in her voice.

"How did you make this?" I asked as she put the finishing touches on another sculpted dessert that looked as if it had come from an architect's drawing board.

She shrugged her shoulders as she gently placed a plump raspberry on top of a swirled dome of whipped cream that looked as if it was really made of white marble.

"It isn't that hard, really," she said as she drizzled thin lines of chocolate syrup around the plate in a design that looked like a tasty spider's web. "You could do it. You draw it out, get it down on paper. Then you calculate. You have to measure everything, make a formula. That's the most serious part of what I do, the measuring. Especially since I can't eat what I make."

"Why not?" I asked, remembering the taste and richness of the last should-be-illegal dessert. I tried to lick my fingers without looking too much like a pig.

"I'm diabetic," she said simply. "Sugar and I get along fine but only from a distance. I have to be careful." She gestured toward one of the other chefs who was working at the opposite end of the kitchen. "Larry helps me with the tasting when I'm not sure or when I'm experimenting."

I stayed by Wendy's side for another hour. Peaches left me to run the truck through some diagnostics (something about a rotor, or maybe it was a radiator) and to fill up the gas tank. I could have stayed in Yancey's kitchen a week, just watching.

Wendy and her creations had me feeling like a kid in Toys Я Us. I listened to her talk about the cakes and the crusts for pies and tarts and flans and brulées and white chocolate and dark chocolate, berries, nuts, and sprinkles and extracts of this, and drops of that. There were influences from here and shades of there and sometimes Wendy sounded like Mr. Dinos in my painting class at the community college. And when she'd finished, she had a work of art rising from a plain white dessert plate.

I knew how to cook and I knew how to bake. I could pinch a pie crust around the edges and ice a cake pretty good. But Wendy's desserts were millions of miles from the ones that I made. I never gave my stuff much thought, just whipped 'em up and threw 'em in whatever pan or plate they needed. Turned the oven on to 350 degrees and wiped my hands. There weren't any complaints. There weren't even any crumbs left when I made a sweet potato pie or a yellow cake with chocolate icing, especially if Mountain was around.

But watching Wendy got me to thinking about cooking in a different way. New words sneaked into my vocabulary like "artistry" and "technique" that didn't come from the last novel I had read. And one more new word: credentials. Could I sculpt a confection onto a plain white plate? Could I craft a pyramid out of chocolate or make custard lighter than clouds and decorate it with a dollop of cream that looked like a marble statue? Could I learn to do that?

Wendy had several framed pieces of paper on the wall of the crowded little corner of a back room that served as her office. These pieces of paper were diplomas and certificates from cooking schools and competitions. She had a row of medallions hanging from red, white, and blue ribbons. She'd baked quiches in Santa Fe and whipped up puddings in a hotel in British Columbia. She had stirred soup in Taipei and baked chocolate confections in Edinburgh. She seemed to have been everywhere and had credentials coming out of her ears.

The question that I wanted to ask got caught in my throat. I had a high school diploma and knew how to use measuring cups and turn on the oven to the right temperature. I knew salt from sugar, cayenne from cumin. I could match the right pot or pan to the recipe. I could stir up fudge in a pan. In other words, my list of "culinary" skills could be added up on five fingers. But I couldn't do puff pastry. I hadn't baked bread or created a soufflé. And I would never think of sculpting whipped cream or cutting out pieces of paper-thin chocolate the way that Wendy did.

I was just a cook. But could I be a . . . chef? I hadn't realized it but I said this aloud.

Wendy laughed.

"Why not?" she said. Without breaking a sweat, she

formed a two-inch-high Babylonian tower of whipped cream on top of strawberry shortcake. I sighed. It was the most beautiful food I'd ever seen. "Sign up for a program. It's as much talent as it is training. You can't have one without the other."

"But I can't speak French!" I exclaimed, remembering the two certificates on her wall from a gourmet academy in Paris.

Wendy shook her head.

"I'm from Tyler, Texas, honey. How much French do you think I spoke when I started in this business? You'll pick up what you need along the way."

Easy for her to say.

I saw chocolate pyramids and white icing skyscrapers in front of my eyes nearly all the way south. I remembered lighter-than-air lemon cake and a dense chocolate cake with a liquid center. I had always stopped to watch Jess work, doing what I called "fancy" cooking as he blackened this, terrined that, or created a pale- and delicate-looking sauce that was packed with flavor out of a little cream, a splash of wine, and a handful of crushed herbs. And I wondered if I could ever transform my homegrown recipes into works of art.

But me? Back to school? I couldn't do that.

You won't know if you don't try, I said to myself. But where would I go? The thought of Juanita Louis and her one-word French vocabulary of "oui" taking cooking lessons in Paris, France? *Girl, I don't think so.* But then, I remembered something. Something stashed in the back of my mind beneath balled-up grocery receipts and my grandmother's pound cake recipe. It was one of those "ruby slippers" moments—the answer was right in front of my face.

One day, late last summer after my painting class at the

community college, I waited to hitch a ride back to Paper Moon with Mignon, who had stopped in to see one of her teachers. I had passed the time by reading the flyers on the bulletin board. It had all kinds of stuff on it: ads for room-mates ("Alternative lifestyles OK"), apartments ("ABSO-LUTELY NO SMOKING AND NO PETS," "Vegans only"), David's Tattoos and Laundromat, and diet pills, contacts for marijuana for medicinal purposes, piercing studios ("Tongues are our specialty"), and the schedules for the next term. The "Food Services Management Depart-ment" announcement was copied onto hot-pink paper. There were courses in restaurant administration, institu-tional food management, and banquet coordination. A deadline for applications to the culinary arts program was set out in bold, black letters. Mignon tapped me on the shoulder, I picked up my portfolio, and we left.

Now the official-looking words on that bulletin board came back to me: "The Culinary Arts Program is accept-ing applicants for its eighteen-month program. Applica-tions may be obtained . . ."

Peaches and I left Los Angeles heading south. It was beautiful but I don't think I saw a damn thing. All I could think about was cooking. Real cooking. And school.

Being a chef was for Jess, it was for Yancey and Wendy. Not for me. The whole idea scared me. Going to school. *Real* school where I would probably be at least a hundred years older than everyone else. Where I would be at least twenty years stupider than everyone else. I talked myself out of the idea as I stared at the road ahead.

Then, Peaches's voice floated into my consciousness. And I said, "Yeah." I have no idea what she said.

"Juanita, are you all right? Is something wrong?"

"Oh, sorry. I'm fine. Just daydreaming," I said.

I imagined a delicate swirl of whipped cream rising above a perfectly cut slice of bourbon sweet potato pecan pie that I had placed in the center of a plain white dessert plate. A plate of perfect little bite-sized somethings tartared in a puff pastry shell, a fairy-sized dollop of mousse on top of each piece. Ah, yes. Horse doovers from Juanita Louis, Chef. You know, that sounded pretty good.

Chapter Three

Heroines in romance novels have a few things in common. They're beautiful, which is probably a good thing. Otherwise the romance part would go out of the window. They are also nineteen years old, but we'll set that aside for now. They're sexy, that goes along with the beautiful part. And they're smart. That's how they figure out how to get out of those situations they get themselves into. But as a newcomer to the romantic heroine game, there's one more thing that I'd like to add to the list: flexibility. If you're going to be a heroine, you have to be able to change course quickly. Make sure your house slippers have rubber soles because you never know when the road will get rocky or the flying carpet you're on will change its direction. Life may turn out the way you've planned—just be ready to change the plan a few times along the way.

We were south of San Diego and headed toward Mexico. Peaches had a few days off after a delivery and wanted to roast on a beach blanket drinking Coronas and listening to Jimmy Buffet. That didn't appeal to me but

visiting Mexico did. I wanted to see the colors and taste
the peppers. I wanted to go to a bullfight, catch a peek at
some Mayan ruins, and listen to the music. You can tell
a lot about folks through their food and their music. I'd
been reading a book about Mexico. And I wanted to try
out my Spanish. I had been practicing.

"A kind of Spanish," Peaches said, frowning after she listened to my attempts. Peaches was decent at conversa-
tional Spanish. She knew all the curse words. But she was
having a hard time getting a handle on Spanish—Juanita-
style.

"Spanish with a spot of central O'hiya mixed in with . . .
what *is* that accent?" Peaches scrunched up her face as she
tried to figure it out. Then she grinned. "Oh, of course,"
she said. "West Virginia."

"Yes, by God," I'd told her proudly. My dad is from
West Virginia and I still have a bit of that twang in my
speech. It sticks to your vowels like caramel sticks to your
teeth. Mix it up with Spanish, though, and you have quite
a sound. It's like putting beef gravy on salmon. It sounds
interesting but it doesn't work.

"Better listen to the tapes again," Peaches said, quickly
pushing the button on my Walkman. "If you pronounce
the words like that, you might get slapped. People will
think you're sayin' something vulgar instead of 'buenos
dias.' "

But there was a sudden change in plans. Paul, one of
Peaches's coworkers, had come down with pneumonia and
was in the hospital. It happened right in the middle of a
job, leaving a shipment in Gila Bend to be picked up.
Peaches checked her maps and turned the Purple Passion
east toward Arizona.

"I'm sorry, Juanita, I know you wanted to see Mexico.

Maybe we can go next month if you want. Bring Jess along, too."

"I'm not worried about it," I told her, and I wasn't. Instead of seeing Mexico, which I'd never seen before, I was going to see Arizona, which I'd never seen before either. I was still coming out ahead.

"When I'm finished in Gila Bend, I'll go north through Phoenix to Utah," Peaches added. "You got the urge to see a salt lake?"

Well, not really, but I did want to see what was so grand about the Grand Canyon and Peaches had said that there were red rocks in Arizona. Since I was used to the brown and gray rocks of Montana that sounded good to me. And that's how I ended up juggling crystals and channeling positive energy in Arizona instead of sipping on a lime in Monterrey. Heroines have to be flexible.

We drove west from San Diego and headed out on I-10, then picked up State Route 85 toward Gila Bend. After the truck was loaded, Peaches's route took us north through Phoenix then into the desert. Along the way, a car the size of a soup can switched lanes without using a turn signal or making sure that there was enough room between it and the semi.

Peaches shifted gears quickly, and then pushed the loud horn of the Kenworth. It sounded like the bellow of a herd of angry elephants. "Son of a bitch! I hope you've got big bumpers on that damn Civic because you're about to get slammed!" she yelled at the tiny little Honda. The engine roared as the truck picked up speed.

I held my breath because that little car had squeezed in with barely six feet between its trunk and the front end of Peaches's rig. Then, the boy flipped her the bird and took off, jumping lanes again to zip past an ancient Ford truck that was struggling along.

"Damn kids," Peaches grumbled. "If you weren't in the cab, I'd . . ."

"No, you wouldn't," I cut her off. "You're too conscientious a driver to go after that young fool. He'll get his, don't you worry."

"Always seems to take too damn long. Where are the Mounties when you need them?" Peaches muttered, pushing the Purple Passion to a few points higher than the legal cruising speed. "Enough of that. Look out the window. Peaches Bradshaw's travelogue is about to begin." She pointed to the right. "That, Miss Juanita, is a bona fide, real, genuine living cactus. Probably a hundred years old or more, which means it's one of the few things older than Millie Tilson." She grinned at her joke. "It's a Saguaro. Pretty neat, huh?"

"Neat" was an all right word but it wasn't enough to describe the cactus. Not nearly enough. There were hundreds of them, all different, something you had to see up close, not ten feet up in the truck cab. When Peaches stopped for gas, I got out to get a better look. There were skinny ones with spidery branches and short fat stubby ones. Some of them looked like little cabbage heads with spikes and others were small and delicate with tiny orange and gold flowers that were too delicate for such a spiky, sharp, little plant. There was also a spindly one with thin branches and lots of spikes. Sometimes, it looked as if it had . . . well, as if it had *moved*. Or, maybe I'd been in the heat too long and was seeing things. When I mentioned this to Peaches, though, she didn't seem surprised.

"Jumping cholla," she said, matter-of-factly. "Folklore

says that the plants *can* move but I wouldn't put much in that."

I hopped away just in case. Didn't want any souvenirs in my butt.

And then, of course, there were the Saguaro, fifty feet tall. Old and majestic with arms raised toward a sun that always shines. I studied each one as we flew by, trying to keep the images branded on my brain. I wondered what dramas these strange giants had seen in their two-hundred-year life spans. The world has surely changed since they first lifted their branches skyward. They watched without expression as folks rode by on horseback, then, in wagons. They watch now as little metal containers whiz by; their expressions still haven't changed. But some of them look gray near the bottom of their trunks. I wonder if we are making them sick. But a hundred years is a long time. Maybe they'll survive us, too.

Thought I'd make myself a cactus garden when I got back to Paper Moon. I would set it up in the south-facing window of the diner. No way was that as much sun as they would get in the desert but cacti are no quitters. They have faith, those plants. They believe in living life in whatever soil or sunshine you find.

When you first see the Sonoran Desert, you think to yourself, "I'm on the moon!" The land seems drab and stark. And empty. It is none of those things. And I didn't expect to like it so much.

It was more colorful than I could have imagined, considering that most of the colors were shades of each other. It was light brown and light tan and dark tan and gold. It was beige and the few spots of fauna were the shade of evergreens and some of the rocks looked white in the sun that never stopped shining. There were pockets of deep mustard yellow and slate gray. Up close, there were dots of white: tiny little flowers that had the nerve to open their faces to heat that could scramble eggs on asphalt. And all of this beauty was set off by a sky that was bluer than turquoise and as bright as a sapphire. The countryside was flat up close and nearly as far as my eyes could see but way off in the distance, I saw a mountain, Humphrey's Peak, it's called, wearing a white cap accessorized by wispy clouds. It looked so cool. I could feel the frost even though I was miles away and it was a hundred degrees in the shade. If there had been any shade. The heat was incredible. Five minutes in this 400-degree oven and I was done.

"It's a dry heat." Peaches repeated the sentiments of every fool I'd ever met who had been in the southwest.

"Dry, my ass," I snapped back. "I don't care how *dry* it is, Peaches, it's *hot!*"

Every drop of moisture in my body was gone; even my tear ducts were empty. You don't sweat in Arizona. You just turn into a pillar of salt like Lot's wife. The water is sucked out of your body the second you step outside. That's why everyone carries a water bottle around. You have to; otherwise you'd have folks passing out on the sidewalks. But it is beautiful. Sculptured and sanded, tough and delicate at the same time. Every plant, animal, and rock are as tough as nails. They have a beauty that is hard to describe. In the heat of the day, the land is quiet and all you hear from the highway are the distant sounds of cars whizzing by on the interstate, the occasional honk of a car horn, and not much else. It's too hot to breathe.

Night is a different story. North of Phoenix, just outside Canyon City, we spent the night in the truck cab. Peaches is like a turtle; she carries her house with her wherever she goes. There are two bunk beds in the back and a small TV. She was trying to drive straight through but her allergies were bothering her and she needed a nap so we stopped. I had already grabbed four or five hours of sleep and once I'm awake, I'm awake. It was four in the morning so I just stayed up, drank a cup of iced coffee, and listened to the sounds of the desert. I was surprised that there were so many.

It is dark out there.

Unless the moon is full, you can't see anything but the stars in the sky. And, except for the occasional passing car, it is quieter than King Tut's tomb on a Wednesday night, as far as human movement goes. But any critter with more than two legs is very busy.

There is constant rustling and the sound of little feet scurrying here and there across the desert floor. Occasionally, you'll hear a yelp and that means there has been some serious trespassing. There's also a squeak now and then and a few yodels. But the scratching and sound of the dry earth crumbling and rocks scattering across a well-worn path are everywhere in the dark. Owls hoot. Once I thought I heard the howl of wolves far off in the distance. The coyote yip and yap then slink away. I know that there are snakes and spiders out here, too, but I try not to think too much about them.

When the night air is very cool, whether it's on Kaylin's Ridge in Montana or in the north central desert of Arizona, you see wonders in the sky. I'd heard that the stars are countless but hadn't really believed it until now. Without clouds or humidity, they cover the deep navy bowl of sky like polka dots on a summer Sunday dress. There are galaxies out there and planets that blink at me.

I wouldn't see this in a city, I couldn't hear the nighttime stories of the lights in the sky. They'd be hidden, masked by the noise and the clouds and the dirt and the lights. I want to see the great cities of the world but I don't think I'd stay very long. I'd miss the quiet songs of the stars too much.

But the dark is lifting. Way off in the distance, east, the first rays of the sun have begun to pierce the inky sky and the glow is like a halo embracing the horizon. Gold and pink, then tangerine, the change happens so slowly, so cleanly that I don't know where night ends and morning begins. Before I can gasp at the beauty of it all, the star of the new day peeks over the foothills and the frantic sounds of scurrying and scratching fade away and melt into the earth. A night owl flies over with one last "who who" as she returns to her nest from a busy evening. And as the day emerges, the desert dissolves into brown, tan and gold, and heat. And silence.

"Do you mind a quick side trip?" Peaches asked me later, after clicking off her cell phone. "We're a little ahead of schedule."

Like I've always said, heroines must be ready for anything.

"No, I don't mind. Where are we going?"

"Sedona. It's west of here but not too far out of our way. I want to get a reading and Nina says she'll squeeze me in."

I have described Peaches as a salt-of-the-earth kind of woman who works hard (driving a semitractor pulling a trailer is not for wimps) and plays hard and takes a no-nonsense look at life. She likes beer, Viceroy cigarettes (although she's trying to quit), football, and ice hockey. But she is superstitious. Very superstitious. She never gets on the road without checking her horoscope, a rabbit's foot hangs from her mirror, and she collects crystals and will not leave the house on a job without her Saint Christopher medal. And he's not even a real saint anymore! Now we are headed northwest toward Sedona, Arizona, where energy vortexes charge up the juices of the local mediums and illuminate auras. These are Peaches's words, not mine. I am just along for the ride.

The desert gives way to more sparse country, almost like the plains in some places but different, brown and tan with little clumps of green here and there. We are moving into canyon country.

To tell the truth, at first, it's not much to look at. In a way, it reminds me of Ohio, where I'm from. The land there is neat and flat. The difference is that in the spring and summer, the fields are green with corn stalks. Out there, the colors are dull and quiet, especially when you compare them to the midday Arizona sky, a sky that's the color of periwinkle flowers on steroids.

Then I see them. I've seen them in bad westerns and good westerns and in truck commercials. I just didn't think they were real.

"Pretty amazing, huh?" My tour guide says as she downshifts.

Yes, they are.

They stretch upward from the bottom of the canyons, hard, full of crags and ridges, red in the sunlight, trying to touch the sky. There is a whole city of these stone cathedrals and in the setting sun, they look as the landscape of some place beyond distance and time must look. Not earthbound at all. Not close.

"People climb 'em," Peaches comments, slowing the truck to a crawl because of the traffic. "Can't understand why . . ." In some ways, Peaches is as earthbound as I am.

But I sure would climb one of those mountains, if I wasn't afraid of heights.

They have their own names—Cathedral, Snoppy, and the names given them when the first woman came along and said, "Wow." A giant took a chisel and hammer and became a sculpting fool. These canyons are her gallery.

We finally reach the quirky little town that has done its best to be a tourist destination and spiritual haven with its tee-shirt shops and crystals, golf courses and spas. The canyon country and Sedona have blended the sublime (one of my new words) with the . . . whatever. I have already seen the sublime. When we meet Peaches's friend, Nina Goldman, I see the "whatever."

Nina's outfit is a combination of hot-pink Indian sari with cargo pants and tank top as accessories. She wears the homeliest sandals that you ever saw—looks like she's walking on straw mats—and has everything pierced that can be. A winding rose bush tattoo curls up her right leg and a labyrinth encircles her navel. She peers at me through glasses that I remember from fifth grade and her bright red hair looks as if someone dropped a large bird nest on it. No one is born with hair this shade of red. Besides Millie Tilson, she is the most original-looking person I've ever seen. Unlike Millie, however, Nina is a flake. Or, to put it in metaphysical terms, she has a few crystals loose and a fuzzy aura.

"Oh, my *God!*" she exclaims as she ushers us into her pavilion, "I am completely undone today, *completely!*" She waves her thin arms everywhere, and almost misses my eye. "I can't believe what's going on! Oh, my Goddess!" She looks like a refugee from a head shop in the late sixties. Actually, that is exactly what she is.

"Peaches, *darling,* I'm happy to see you. I'm so sorry that things are such a mess! I'm drowning, just gasping for a breath! *Gasping!*" Nina nearly chokes as she races through her words, running her sentences together one right after another without taking a breath. I can't keep up. She hugs Peaches then steps back to give her a once-over. "Ohhhh . . . your aura is brown with mustard yellow around the perimeter, not good. Not good at all. I'll do your cards and we'll see what's going on." She smiles at me. Then she nods. "Nice to meet you, Juanita. Make yourself at home, please." She gestures toward the mounds of huge pillows scattered around the floor. Then she studies me with a squint as if she is looking through a microscope. "Purple, yes, very good. Do you want some tea?"

Purple what?

I watch them disappear into the deep red paisley-papered room that Nina uses as her channeling studio. You can't imagine a bigger contrast: Nina, a retro-fashionista, and laid-back Peaches, who wears tee shirts, baseball caps, and painters pants most of the time. Did I mention the blue Converse All Star sneakers?

Nina told me to make myself at home, so that's what I did. Snooped around.

Nina's house is one of those modern things with lots of windows and more halls than rooms. It's built in an architectural style that I probably couldn't pronounce. *Very* high eyebrow. Somebody has to explain it to you and make you understand that it's all that and a bag of corn chips. But as far as I'm concerned, it's like the emperor and his new clothes. I don't care what they say; his highness is only wearing a jockstrap.

One thing about Nina, though. She is an equal opportunity decorator. Her decorating style is, literally, from

one extreme to the other. In some of the rooms, the walls
are white, the furniture, if there is any, is white, and the
floors are tile or slate. The rugs hang on the walls like pictures. Oh, they're white, too. Not too much you can say
about an all-white room, is there?

In the other rooms, your mind can't process all of
the colors, textures, beadings, paisleys, plaids, and fringes:
Japanese nearly nothing to Victorian everything everywhere. Huge colorful beaded pillows in bright greens,
blues, reds, and golds are scattered across the Oriental
rugs that Nina has used to cover the floors. Beaded curtains jingle when you pass through them—Nina uses them
instead of doors—and she's draped deep rose-colored cloth
with gold threads in it across the ceilings so that the ma-
terial floats along like clouds from one end of the room
to the next. Carvings of elephants made out of teak, jade
Buddhas set in little grottos, and an interesting brass figure
with many arms take up space with brass incense burners,
candleholders, and stacks and stacks of books. I guess I like
the colorful room better. It reminds me of a book that I
read about Scheherazade. Or was it the book about the
Algerian brothel? I can't remember which.

It's a pretty house but you get a little turned around with
all of the different levels and the blank walls that all look
alike and the angles. If I were a spirit, I wouldn't like being
channeled into a house that you need a road map for. I
took a couple of wrong turns before I found my way back
to the room where Nina and Peaches had left me. It was
good timing because they were just coming out of the
"channeling studio" when I walked in.

"I'm sure it will all work out," Peaches said.

"Something wrong?" I asked, being nosy again.

"Just a life-or-death, heart-stopping *crisis*," Nina gasped out in a dramatic voice. "My cousin ran off to get married and she's honeymooning in the South Pacific. For four weeks!" Nina's heavily lined eyes blinked. I think they were filled with emotion. "My focus is soooo fractured now!"

"Nina rents out rooms and the guesthouse on the ridge just behind the house . . ." Peaches started to explain.

"It helps with the expenses when the energy vortex weakens and my readings fall off," Nina interrupted.

Peaches rolled her eyes.

"Two thousand dollars a week is good help if you can get it."

Nina poured pale green liquid into a Chinese teacup and handed it to Peaches.

"Better get used to this."

Peaches took a sip, gulped hard, and made a face. Now she looked as green as the tea. She sat down quickly.

"My cousin is my partner. Now she's in Bali or Tahiti or some island in the typhoon belt." Nina sighed dramatically. "My aura is brown, I just *know* it."

"Maybe you should meditate more," Peaches volunteered. She set down the cup of tea.

Nina shook her head.

"This cooking stuff blocks my energy paths!" Nina exclaimed, waving her navy-blue painted nails in the air. "The spirits do not enter a distracted mind!"

"Did someone say 'cooking'?" I asked.

"Yes," Nina wailed. But she wasn't completely distracted. She picked up Peaches's teacup and passed it back to her. Peaches made another face. "My cousin, who is my business partner, does the cooking. I don't know what I'm going to do! I can boil tea and pour oatmeal but that's it!"

The "New Age" lifestyle is all right for readings, crystals, and music but doesn't work for cooking. Hard to channel spirits while you're pouring oatmeal.

Peaches noticed my expression because she stood up fast.

"Oh, no you don't!" She put up her hands as she warned me off. "Put the idea right out of your head! If I leave you here, Jess will fry me up and feed me to the bears! Besides, I thought you wanted to go to the Grand Canyon! What about Mexico?"

"The Canyon isn't going anywhere, is it?" I asked. "I'm still going to Mexico. It isn't that far from here. I'm just taking a little . . . vacation, a . . . sabbatical." One of my new words had come in handy.

Peaches groaned. Nina was so happy that she almost wet her sari.

She hugged the air out of me and gushed in her dramatic, nasally voice.

"I am soooo relieved! I can feel my aura changing nooow. *Namaste,* dahling, *namaste.*" She clasped her hands together and bowed from the waist.

I seem to attract interesting people.

Peaches rolled her eyes and sighed loudly.

"Jess will cook my kidneys for this," she grumbled.

But it was a good bargain.

I was paid a nice little chunk of cash. I got a beautiful room that faced east. The sun woke me up every morning, and off in the distance I could see the foothills and the red rock cathedrals. It was a surprise to me that Nina had decorated the room in a, well, normal way. The furniture was streamlined and beautiful, Mission-style, she called it, and the sheets were so soft.

"Five hundred thread count or higher, that's all I buy," Nina said. Whatever that means—more threads somewhere, I guess.

I got a discount with some of the other consultants in town (according to Nina, the word "psychic" isn't used anymore), ten percent off a chakra-balancing clinic, and twenty percent off a past-life regression. My aura cleansings Nina did for free.

"The color of ripening irises," she said. "Bee-yoo-ti-full." She fixed her brown eyes on me. "But you're coming to a crossroads. You are going to have to make some important decisions really soon."

It isn't easy being purple.

I got all of these goodies for doing practically nothing.

Now, I've cooked breakfast for forty people or more in two hours: eggs, bacon, sausage, grits, hash browns, pancakes, and French toast. But throwing together wheat toast (unbuttered) and black coffee or a fruit cup and a few "lean" turkey and sprouts sandwiches for executive types who work out at a gym for two hours a day (So, what is the point of a vacation?) or dieting divas who only eat the grapes out of the fruit cup was not what I would call real work. By ten o'clock in the morning, I was finished with all of the cooking and the cleanup. First time I've had a vacation in . . . well, it's the first time I've *had* a vacation!

But I am not cut out for being a lady of leisure. Not that I didn't try real hard.

I'd never had a massage before but I'd seen them on TV and Nina raved about them. So, I took advantage of a fifteen-percent-off coupon and had a massage. That was a big mistake, the discount *and* the massage. I guess I'm a prude at heart. I don't mind nakedness and other things but I don't think you have to parade them around, know what I mean? I don't feel comfortable showing my backside to just anyone. Jess likes my butt (says I have dimples) but that's for another paragraph. Anyway, I was trying to be cool about letting everything I usually have covered up hang out but I was no good at it. I felt like I was blushing all over and had to count to a thousand or so to keep from jumping off that table in a panic and covering myself up in the XXXL-sized robe. The other problem? By the time Leilani finished chopping my back and kneading my arms and legs like bread dough that had Silly Putty in it, I felt as if I'd been assaulted. I was so sore that I could barely raise my arm the next morning to grab the cinnamon from the cabinet! Maybe the fifteen percent that I *didn't* pay was for the "therapeutic values" of the massage. Sometimes it's just better to pay full price.

Another week, I decided to be a pool bunny. Nina's house has a swimming pool in the back surrounded by little grottoes and decorated with beautiful plants and flowers. Her water bill must be a bitch. It's away from the road so it's private and very quiet, just the kind of place that a lady of leisure like me would enjoy. I decided to relive my teenaged years in Columbus. KayRita and I used to go to the Maryland pool (Momma had bought us matching swimsuits) just to see the cute boys and try to catch the eye of the lifeguards. Neither one of us could swim, but that wasn't the point. Looking cute in a bathing suit was.

So, I pulled out the black swimsuit I'd bought from Target, a snappy little number with control panels and a support bra built in, and sashayed out to the cabana with a beach towel and a stack of things to read.

I settled myself on one of the cushioned loungers and

tried to relax. I watched the ripples in the pool when one of Arizona's few breezes blew by. I listened to the birds calling. I flipped through the latest issue of a magazine dedicated to women who can wear Band-Aids for underwear and opened a mystery that I'd bought. I lasted a half hour. Lounging around a pool is not for me: It's too quiet, too hot, and there's too little to do.

My second week in Sedona, I shared poolside with the television actress who was staying in the guesthouse. Since I had fixed her a lunch of romaine lettuce, vinaigrette, and pine nuts and iced green tea, I wasn't surprised that she was lying around the pool. Romaine lettuce doesn't give you enough energy to do much else.

Now *she* knew how to be a lady of leisure. Jacki Francis was her name and she was an early-thirty-something, the size of a toothpick with cantaloupes for breasts and a flat behind. She sunbathed topless. I admired her for being able to do that. If I tried that stunt, there'd be an earthquake. We chitchatted on and off between her browsing the Revlon ads in *Vogue* and me turning the Arcadia Valley Community and Technical brochures around and around in my hands.

Jacki had been a little snippy with me at first but once she learned that I got a choice table at Yancey's on twenty-four hour's notice without a reservation, she was all smiles and sugar.

She pulled down her dark pink sunglasses and studied me as if I had just flown in from Jupiter.

"Cool. Yancey's. You must really have connections. Only the A-list of celebrities can get a table there without a reservation."

I smiled back at her. If you're on the A-list, you don't have to say anything.

After that, Jacki and I got to be as close as fuzz on a peach. She probably wanted me to get her a table at Yancey's.

"We're on hiatus," she told me after I asked her what she was doing in Sedona. She sighed dramatically. *Very well done*, I thought. "I needed some head time off. You know, to restore my spirit."

I thought of the Belgian waffle with berries that I had made for her for breakfast a few days ago. Jacki had taken two bites of the waffle and picked off four of the blueberries. If I was going to restore *my* spirit, I'd need a lot more food in my stomach than that.

I was having enough trouble on a full stomach trying to get through the application packet for the culinary arts program at Arcadia Valley Community and Technical.

The teachers had initials behind their names. They were "Master Chefs" and "Chefs de Cuisine" and "Culinary Fellows." They had studied in London and Paris and New York. Not Dave's Coney Island or Peggy's Steak and Stop but restaurants that had lots of diamonds and stars below their names, restaurants that were located all over the world. These chefs had won awards for culinary excellence. I could pronounce "excellence" but "culinary" still got me tongue-tied. In the photos, they wore white coats and tall hats. The class list was not what I was expecting, either. I had thought, maybe "Baking 101" or "How to Keep Your Soufflés from Falling Down and Your Pie Crusts from Rising Up." Instead, there was "Business Mathematics," "Food and Beverage Cost Control," and "English Composition." I closed the booklet. Maybe the admissions office had sent me the wrong course list.

But the potential pay was many times more than I had ever made in my whole life. And, for whatever reason, there is a shortage of nurses and a shortage of trained chefs with credentials. Maybe I could go to the South of France, Australia, New York, Scottsdale, Sonoma Valley . . . little old Juanita Jackson Louis from Columbus, Ohiya, living extra-large in California wine country. I could manage a dining room. I could teach. That picture made me smile. I could go anywhere or do anything that I wanted. I would have a . . . profession.

Like the Scarecrow in *The Wizard of Oz*, I could only do so much with the cooking I was used to and with mother wit. "If I only had a brain . . ." Both the Scarecrow and I found out that it wasn't the "brain" at all. What we didn't have was the diploma.

Ok, I'll fill out the application. I don't have anything to lose, I told myself. *It'll make me feel better, at least I will have tried. Besides, I won't get in anyway.* I pulled out one of my three-for-a-dollar, fifty-cent ink pens.

I glanced over at Jacki. She'd turned over. I guess her front side was done.

"To restore my spirit," she'd said.

I didn't need any spirit restoration; Paper Moon had done that for me. But what are you supposed to do with a restored spirit? It was a question that I asked myself over and over again as I filled out the application. Eventually, I did get some answers.

I just didn't expect to get so many of them.

Chapter Four

After one week at Nina's, I started making suggestions. Just little ones. Nina did all right but some of the little things that Millie did at the B&B had made an impression on me. Cool towels for the pool when it was hot, warm ones for the chilly desert nights, a trimmed-down menu for the trim size zero types who stayed with her. (Why buy pancake mix for folks who don't eat pancakes?) I'd told her to think about giving the rooms names to match the decor. Nina liked that idea—Suite Four became "The Elephant Suite" because of its Indian decor and row of antique mahogany elephants, and Room Two became "The Dove Room," in honor of the doves who'd nested just outside the window, waking up the guests with their morning cooing.

Millie slipped a *Paper Moon Gazette* onto the breakfast trays. It wasn't a real newspaper, just a 4-1-1 on the doings in town and the surrounding areas. Millie even included a catalogue for Bob's Shop 'n Play, a bait shop combined with an adult bookstore, for guests who'd forgotten to bring their own videos or fishing tackle. I didn't think Nina had to go that far but she appreciated the idea and started cranking out *Nina's Nuggets* for her guests.

By the fourth week, I was hardly cooking at all because (a) Nina's guests barely ate and (b) I was too busy taking reservations, managing the housekeeping staff, and pulling together tidbits for Nina's newsletter. Nina's readings had picked up.

"Darling, I'm exhausted. Just ground to pencil dust!" If she wasn't giving a reading she was recovering from one. "So much negativity!" she'd exclaim.

"Nothing Metamucil can't cure," I'd mumble out of her hearing.

Nina and I disagreed on this point. It's not that I don't believe in spirits, I do. But I just thought that the folks who'd come to Nina needed to try a laxative first. They may be full of evil spirits. Or they may be full of something else.

Out of the blue, Nina said, "Darling, my cousin's not coming back. She's moving to New Zealand with her new husband."

Nina was calm when she said this, which surprised me. I expected a "Oh, my Goddess!" or something like it.

Her eyes, through a pair of cranberry-red eyeglasses trimmed in rhinestones, probed my face.

"Have you ever thought about going into the inn-keeping business, Juanita?"

Yeah, I had . . .

In true Nina-style, she did not give me time to answer.

"You'd be mah-va-lous here, just mah-va-lous. I did the cards last night. We'll be partners. You manage the inn part of the business, I handle the psychic stuff, and we share the rest. What d'you say?"

"Wait up, Nina!" She was talking ten miles a minute. Business? Partners? "You're goin' way too fast, girl. I don't know nothin' about running a business." I thought about Jess's receipts and spreadsheets and appointments with the accountant in Missoula. Me, I just wanted to cook.

"It's nothing!" Nina exclaimed, with a snap of her ever-changing nails now polished a tangerine shade called "Tropical Orange Freeze Punch." "You'd pick it up just like that!"

"But what about your cousin?"

Nina shrugged and a tinkling sound filled the room. Nina wears armloads of bangle bracelets, long dangling earrings in her double-pierced ears, and tiny little silver bells on her ankle bracelets. You can hear her coming and going. When she breathes, it sounds like a choir of wind chimes with cow bells keeping the beat.

She gave me a look that was very un-Nina like. It was steady, unblinking, and wise.

"I've offered to buy her out," she answered in a calm, low-pitched, businesslike tone. "My attorney's drawing up the papers. If she accepts, the deal could close by the end of May."

She pushed a very thick heavily printed document across the desk toward me. I didn't try to read it. Except for the numbers that followed the dollar sign.

"You're the best thing that's happened to me since tarot cards, darling," Nina continued. "Reservations are up, the word of mouth has been very productive, and your inventory control enhancements have markedly improved the bottom line. A fifteen percent savings on food alone! I just needed someone to keep things organized!"

Inventory control enhancements? Bottom line? Who was this woman?

"But I can't operate the hacienda by myself," she continued. "Once I get the buyout wrapped up, I want you to work with me." Nina's four-tiered chandelier earrings danced around her swanlike neck. "You have the talent, darling, and a real aptitude for this work."

I slid the intimidating papers back to her.

"You want me to work for you? Take Butterfly's place as the cook full-time?" That didn't surprise me. I am a good cook and Nina's guests seemed to agree, the few times any of them had eaten enough food to count for anything.

Nina's answer surprised me.

"Noooo, darling, not as the cook. Weren't you *listening*? As my *partner*. My spirit guide, Ramona, says it'd be a good idea for us to go into business *together*."

Well, *namaste*, darling.

Ever hear people talk about their lives turning upside down? You would think that my life flip-flopped like that when I left the Midwest and ended up in Montana. Or that it happened when I met Jess or later when I took off with Peaches to see the Pacific Ocean. I thought that too, once. But I was wrong.

My life flip-flopped while I was in Arizona.

The "consulting position" that I took with Nina started out as four weeks that stretched out to six, then a few months—and I squeezed as much into it as I could with two weeks here in Arizona, up to Salt Lake City, down to Tucson, with three weeks in Paper Moon in between. I visited Chaco Canyon—big, mysterious. I took a donkey tour of the Grand Canyon—bigger and more mysterious. I peeked over the edge of the Canyon, arm wrestling with my fear of heights all the way. I was amazed. The tiny thread of blue-black silk that was the Colorado River

wound its way through the canyons like a decorative ribbon through the hair of Mother Earth. Beautiful. I mean,
what else can you say?

Peaches was impatient.

"Tell Nina to get someone else because I'm picking you
up in two weeks," Peaches bellowed over her cell phone.
"Nina's one of those give 'em an inch, take four miles people. Jess gave me hell the last time I was there and I don't
intend to go through that again."

But I wasn't worried about Jess. He just growls sometimes just to see if he still can.

"If you're in the mood to cook that badly, you might as
well come back to Paper Moon before I run off all the customers," Jess grumbled. "Fish Reynolds nearly took my skin
off, complainin' about the tuna salad. 'It ain't good like
Juanita's. Tastes like you forgot something.'" Jess mim-
icked Fish's flat, tweedy voice. "I told him if he wants to
have Juanita's tuna salad, he'd better head to Arizona and
fast."

I laughed. Jess and I had this conversation a lot. Whenever we talked, I had to remind him of some ingredient
that he had forgotten. It was either the tuna salad, or the
meatloaf, or the sweet potatoes.

"You forgot to add sugar to the tuna salad," I accused
Jess.

"Juanita, it just don't seem right adding something sweet
to a bowl full of flaked tuna. It's against the Gospels."

"You didn't add it, did you?" I said. I couldn't help but
grin. A long pause. I could see Jess's jaw set like a boulder
in a mountain.

"No. And I didn't put maple syrup in the sweet potatoes
either." He sounded proud of that.

"I'll bet Mountain had something to say about that."
I could see Mountain now, shoveling my sweet potato
casserole into his mouth with a ham-sized hand and getting the marshmallows all over his top lip.

"Yes, he did. You get your aura read yet?"

"It's the color of fresh-picked irises. Deep purple."

"Humph. Must be those hormone pills," Jess countered.
"I miss you, Miz Louis."

"I miss you, Mr. Gardiner."

And I did miss him. But not once did that man say,
"Come home, Juanita, and stop this foolishness," or try to
make me feel bad because he missed me.

"You got things to do, you go do 'em. I'll be here when
you get back," he'd told me when I left. "Course, the diner
might not have any customers left . . ."

I liked to take long walks and, sometimes, if it wasn't
too hot, I meandered up the trails in Boynton Canyon and
nearly cracked my neck looking up at the cliffs. That's
how I think things over, just put one foot in front of the
other—away from cars and noise and people and their
nonsense. I walk along the edge of a small canyon and
study the red rocks. Sometimes, I think I can hear them
hum. I have a theory about mountains and red rocks and
rolling hills and thick, dense forests: God put them there
to break up our line of sight so that we can't see too far
ahead.

The phone call came in the morning before breakfast.

I wasn't any damn good the rest of the day. I threw out
the omelet I made, burned the bacon to a black, nasty crisp,
and put hot sauce on the French toast instead of maple
syrup. After I mixed up a batch of chicken salad using yellow mustard instead of mayonnaise, I called it quits. I just
couldn't think about food anymore.

Millie Tilson was dead.

I'd seen her last at Thanksgiving when I was in Paper Moon, Millie and her seventy-year-old "boy toy." The town was still in an uproar about it. I think it might have been the age difference, as if any of us had been able to figure out what that *was.* Millie's family had been sworn to secrecy.

"Juanita, she would skin me like a red deer if I told you," her nephew, Horace Patterson, had admitted sheepishly.

Millie had been enjoying herself. She and Doc Hessenauer loved to gamble and went to Las Vegas for long weekends. They raced their convertibles (she in the Caddy, he in a neon yellow Boxster) on a small, out-of-the-way stretch of State Route 35 at the speed of light. Horace, a state trooper, could never catch them. They enjoyed "clubbing," but that wasn't easy in Paper Moon. The only place that loosely qualified as a "nightclub" was Em's Place at the northern edge of town and that was because it was open at night and sold beer. So, Millie and the Doc spent Christmas in Cancun and New Year's Eve in Palm Springs with friends from her Texas days. Montana was way too "provincial" for them. I like that word. I'll have to look it up.

"I want to go at lightning speed," she'd told me once when she was in a philosophical mood. "Out in a flash, no lingering around in the hospital with bedpans or those morphine drips." She'd waved her arms and the white boa-trimmed silk gown swished. "On to the next journey like the snap of a finger!" And she popped those well-manicured fingers loudly to emphasize her point. "And Juanita," she instructed me, her eyes sharp, her expression serious. "Make sure that they do my nails and touch up my roots. I don't want people looking into the casket whispering about how bad my hair looks! I'd like to be wearing my white Mainbocher suit, too, if you think you can remember."

Maine sashay? Maine bockshay? Whatever. I didn't like the direction the conversation was taking so I quickly agreed to what Millie was telling me. I told her that I would remember to get her to shut up. I just didn't think I would need to remember so soon.

She and the Doc had been taking tango lessons.

"I did the tango with General Peron once in Buenos Aires, the old fascist, but that was a few years ago," Millie had said. "The Doc and I are talking about taking a cruise around Latin America."

One of her two-inch heels skidded on the polished floor at the dance studio and Millie went down. She wasn't much bigger than a half second anyway and those bones cracked like dry twigs. It had to hurt but Millie laughed it off, at least that's what the Doc said, until she tried to get up. That's when he called the EMS squad.

"All of that fuss!" Millie had told me later. She was very annoyed. "The noise and those damn lights blinking off and on. Such a to-do!"

After the surgery, she couldn't get up and move around right away (and not for lack of trying, you know Millie), so the bedpan became a part of her daily beauty ritual. "The ultimate indignity, Juanita," she'd said. It was one of the few times that I ever heard her sigh or heard anything close to resignation in her voice.

Millie was the patient from hell. People who have never been flat on their backs in their lives don't take to hospitals. Four days in the hospital, four and a half weeks at a rehabilitation extended-care facility ("Extended-care facility, my wrinkled ass," Millie had grumbled. "It's a damn

old folks' home!"), and then back to Paper Moon with a
nurse. She would have spent more time in the rehab center but was discharged early. I later learned she was put out
"due to bad behavior." *Her* bad behavior. It wasn't the
wheelchair races in the halls or the poker games in the
sunroom that were the problem, so Millie explained to me
later, probably leaving out most of the bad stuff she'd
done. But she'd had Inez smuggle in Turkish cigarettes
and the fixings for her favorite drink, the Bourbon Old-
Fashioned, so that when her surgeon made his two-week
postsurgical visit and found his patient puffing away and
sipping on a cocktail, well, you can just imagine. Millie
said that his eyes bulged and his ears flapped out as if they
were going to turn into wings and take off—without his
head!

"I think the man had an apoplectic fit," Millie wrote me.
"He told me that I shouldn't mix the alcohol with my medi-
cations. I informed him that I *wasn't* mixing them since I
took the pills well before cocktail hour."

She graciously accepted her expulsion and went home,
promising, with her fingers crossed behind her back, to
behave herself and suspend her cocktail hours until she
was completely off the heavy-duty Tylenol.

Besides deciphering Millie's letters like an archaeologist
trying to read Egyptian hieroglyphics for the first time, I
got to hear about it all from Jess, Inez, and Barb, the nurse
who was taking care of Millie. Millie was not the kind of
woman to lie around the house and get well eventually.
She wanted everything to happen right now. She'd threatened poor Dr. Novak with malpractice if he didn't have
her up and salsa dancing by Easter because she and the
Doc had "plans." They were off to Palm Springs for Valen-
tine's Day and she had already bought her ticket and

didn't want the money to go to waste. But the going was slow: a wheelchair, a walker, and, then, a cane. She had to sit down a certain way and sleep only on her side. She limped and, worse than anything, I think, she couldn't wear the high heels or the filmy nylons that she loved. They had been replaced by low-heeled, sensible block-looking clodhoppers and thick, milky-looking white support hose. Millie was mortified. "Ugliest damn things you ever saw!" She was hobbling back to life and, even though we didn't say it aloud, she hoped, as we all did, that she'd hobble fast enough to outrun the things that could hurt her.

Maybe Millie saw it coming.

"Juanita," she'd written in a handwriting that had lots of bows, whooshes, and exclamation marks, "old age can't catch you if you keep moving. I see him peeking around my door. I have to get rid of this cane!"

But sometimes, it's the little things that get you. Little things like germs. It was cold and flu season and Paper Moon was hit as bad as anyplace else. Sedona got it, too; not even the crystals could protect us. Folks passed it around like a handshake after church. It was a sticky little sucker and some people got it twice. It was so bad that it took on a life of its own. Jess, who never gets sick, came down with it and coughed for nearly a month. He referred to it with a sneer as "the Cold."

"The Tilsons are as strong as oxen even though we don't look like it," Millie had bragged to me once. "We survived ice storms in Minnesota and drought on the eastern plains of Montana. It takes a lot to take out a Tilson."

No, it only took one little germ.

"The Cold" came back like a bad check. It brought a

lot of nasty stuff with it. Millie started coughing and the cough moved southward into her chest. The antibiotics made her sick and then she got a temperature. She had to go back to bed and got too weak to use her cane or even the walker anymore. Her temperature kept spiking, one hundred, one hundred and three, and then back to one hundred. Millie tossed, turned, and sang. She spoke to people who weren't there. Asim, the Siamese cat, kept watch.

Finally, after two weeks of touch and go, Barb felt comfortable enough to let her patient sleep alone in the room. Millie's temperature had broken and she wasn't coughing as much. For the first time in a few days, Millie wasn't delirious.

"Barbara, you've been a good girl," Millie had told her. "You go and grab a nap. I am not going anywhere." But she lied about that.

At midnight, Barb checked on her patient and found that she was in a peaceful and final sleep. The Siamese cat, who had hardly left her side during her illness, gave Millie one last look, then jumped from the bed and slinked out the door. Inez says that cat has hardly been seen since.

"Can you get away?" Jess asked. "The funeral is on Wednesday afternoon."

"There's no 'can' to it," I barked out, not angry at him, angry at Millie for leaving me without a fairy godmother. "I'll let you know after I've checked the flights."

"Number 1695, United, leaves Flagstaff at 8:15 Tuesday for Denver, change planes and take number 1141. It gets into Missoula at 12:30. Be on it, you have an e-ticket. I'll pick you up from the airport."

I love this man. He is always laying down red carpet to soften my steps.

I remembered something.

"Call Inez. And ask her to find a white Maine Bocker suit. Millie said that she wanted . . ." I couldn't finish.

"I'll call her," Jess interrupted. "Take a walk, Juanita."

Nina was sympathetic. She said she'd felt a weakening in Millie's energy. "You've been doing me a huge favor. Do what you have to do. Spirit said that you would be going home soon. I'm really sorry to hear about Millie." She frowned for a moment as if she was thinking about something. "But don't worry about her. She made it to the other side all right."

Probably taking more tango lessons, I thought. And just the idea of Millie dancing a steamy tango in the hereafter with some dashing man made me smile.

Peaches called from the road. She had a delivery in Needles but had to get back to Casper for a doctor's appointment and couldn't come to the funeral.

Doctor's appointment? Warning bells started going off in my head. Peaches hadn't looked right the last time she rode through Sedona. She was thinner, her face was pale, and she seemed to be moving slow—not like Peaches at all.

"Must be my new diet," she said.

"Peaches, what's going on? Are you all right?"

"Fine, fine, just routine annual stuff, you know. Getting all the plumbing checked and everything." She really did sound happy even with the roaring engine in the background. But something made me think that there was something that Peaches wasn't telling me. Was it intuition? God, I hoped that it wasn't anything serious, something else to worry about.

"OK, if you say so," I told her. "Don't let me find out there's something wrong with you, girl. I'll kick your behind."

Peaches's laughter was cut off by coughing. I knew that she'd quit smoking. But had she quit too late?

"How you getting to Montana?" she yelled. I heard the Purple Passion's horn blasting.

"Flying. Please say a prayer," I said.

"I wish that I could be there," she yelled over the crackling cell phone connection. "Always liked Millie, she was a good old broad. A little nutty but all right."

In Peaches-speak, "all right" meant that Millie was almost perfect.

I took a walk.

Nina's place backs up against the foothills just outside Sedona near a little ridge—like the way Jess's cabin sets up on Kaylin's Ridge. But that's where the similarities end. Jess's cabin is almost hidden by forest. It's not that far from the diner but it might as well be on the other side of the world. It is surrounded by giant trees and every four-legged creature that you can imagine. Whenever there is a knock on the door, I think it's a brown bear outside wanting to come in for a cup of coffee.

The hills outside Sedona are crumbly and rocky with scraggly bushes and stubborn cacti hanging onto a spoonful of water. There are hardly any trees at all. There's a path that folks 'round here say led to a mine but I don't see that, unless they were digging for gravel. It's worn down, so lots of feet have used it but not for any gold or tin or any other ore that some poor soul thought these little hills could give up. They ain't fooling me. They trudged up here for the same reason that I did—the view.

I found me a spot just perfect for my behind where I could lean against a boulder and rest my back. I looked down on the town sprawled along the highway. And off in the distance, I saw the red rocks gleaming in the late morning sunshine. It's a beautiful and peaceful spot and sometimes I would nestle against the rock and close my eyes. (After checking for snakes first.) Besides the back porch of the diner that overlooks Arcadia Lake, I think this is one of my favorite places.

Used to be, a long time ago—in another life, as Nina would say—I was afraid of places like this. Open places, spaces where hills bury their toes into the earth, where the fingertips of the mountains tickle the sky. I'd stand on the back porch of Jess's diner and look out at Arcadia Lake and wonder what Kaylin's Ridge was like but was too scared to go there. I'd been used to tiny places with tight boundaries. I knew fences and barriers and right angles. The openness of the plains, the never-ending green of the forest with its splotches of gold sunshine beneath my feet, I didn't know these things until I came west. The land, the people, people like Millie, all of these things. Before I knew Millie I thought I needed rooms to be safe. Thought I needed small places and small ideas to go with them.

It's all turned upside down on me now. I don't like cities, I don't like traffic, I don't give a damn about nice shopping. Give me a vast grassy plain, a mountain or two, a little desert for spice, and a cool forest of towering pines. From afraid of spaces to afraid of fences, that's me. And now, I needed the canyon's depth to think, the nosebleed section of the red rock's highest point to mourn.

And so, I'm here with my butt settled into place, wiping my eyes and balling up tissues and wondering why I'm crying over a woman who I've only known a short time— an old broad who never met a challenge she didn't accept or see a roadblock that she didn't go around. And even the prospect of death—like everything else—didn't scare Millie. She was just afraid that it would inconvenience her.

"Doesn't frighten me one damn bit, except . . ." she'd told me the last time I saw her. This was when she was on the mend from the broken hip and hobbling around on a cane. "Except that I have so much planned! The cruise next year and the Doc and I were thinking about Alaska. Did you know that I spent some time in Alaska? Ketchikan." Her sapphire-blue eyes sparkled with mischief.

"Millie, nothing you say ever surprises me," I'd told her. But I could not imagine her wearing those sheer negligees in Ketchikan. When I told her that, she smiled impishly.

"I wore less than that! It's *amazing* how warm a log fire can be. I have so much to do. If only we could have death by appointment. Then, maybe, I could work everything in."

A scratching sound caught my attention, pulling me away from the memory and my tears. A pair of rabbits scampered up the hill, stopped, looked at me as if I owed them last month's rent, then hopped away.

At eighty plus, which is all she'd ever admit to, Millie had so much to do, so many plans. Going on forty-five, I was afraid to make any. Scared that something would go wrong. Scared that I would fail.

I heard the screech of a hawk above me farther up the ridge. From the sound of things, it had lunch on its mind and was preparing to make the pickup. That's focus for you.

"I can't do that," I would tell Millie when she would suggest that I try this or go there.

Her deep blue eyes would darken for a moment then narrow and her face would take on a serious expression.

"Of course you can," she would snap back. "Don't tell yourself that you can't and don't pay attention to anybody *else* who has small ideas about what you can do. If I'd listened to every damn fool who told me I couldn't do something, or shouldn't do something, I wouldn't get out of bed in the morning. It's amazing how much you can get accomplished if you don't give a damn about what other people think."

Millie was the kick-in-the-ass, get-up-off-your-behind match striker that I needed to push me into the arena with the lions. She didn't take prisoners and she didn't listen to excuses.

" 'Shit or get off the pot.' That's what they used to say," she'd say in a voice sharp as a whip.

Yeah, that's what they used to say all right.

Now she was gone.

I looked out across the ridge, past the town and the canyon, toward the red rocks. I tried to feel the vortex but I didn't. I dabbed my eyes and blew my nose and prayed that the red rocks could spare just a little bit of energy for me.

Too soon I was sitting in a cylinder made of steel and other heavy things zooming through space at an altitude high enough to make your nose bleed. If God had meant for folks to fly, wouldn't he have made us with wings? I was on an airplane from Flagstaff to Missoula, headed to Paper Moon, Montana, just off I-90, east of Montana State Route 93, and at least thirty miles from anything else. When it comes to Paper Moon, it doesn't matter where you are coming from, you can't get there from anywhere.

The captain's voice came over the loudspeaker. Cheerfully, he told us that we were flying through the jet stream so there might be a "little turbulence." Yeah, right. The next "little" bump nearly threw me into the seat of the young man next to me who had a spike in his nose. I had been wondering where else he had spikes.

"Oh, excuse me," I muttered, trying to get situated again and keep from wetting my pants. He grinned and said, "That's cool." Lord, he had a spike in his tongue, too.

The plane swooped down beneath the clouds then banked to the left as it made the approach to Missoula International. It was a bumpy ride down but I didn't notice the turbulence this time. I stared out the window at the snow and the patches of brown here and there, the ribbons of gray and white that snaked between. In another two hours, I would be in Paper Moon.

Chapter Five

I didn't know how much I missed Paper Moon until Jess turned off at Exit 12A, Silver Spring Road. There's no silver and there's no spring. Somebody just thought that would be a nice name for a road. There is nothing like the cool, dark green of a western Montana forest and the beauty of the sunlight warming the snow-covered surface of Arcadia Lake. It was still winter and Montana wouldn't throw off the cold and the snow for at least two months. Winter here is the real deal and not for sissies. There were several feet of snow on the ground and the wind felt as if it was visiting with relatives from the Arctic Circle.

I stuck my nose out the window. The icy air froze my lungs and made me cough. It felt good. I smiled, closed my eyes, and enjoyed it.

"Juanita, that desert has dried out your brains," Jess commented. "Only the dog hangs his head out the window. What's the matter with you? Silly woman," he murmured. "Move your head."

I pulled my head back in and he raised the window. I snuggled into the multilayered coat that Jess had brought for me to wear. I had a winter coat, but Jess said it wouldn't keep a buffalo's butt warm. "An Ohio coat," Jess called it, not heavy enough for the winters out here.

We'd been riding in silence since Missoula. I was in a thoughtful mood. Jess would glance over at me once in a while, probably to see if I was still awake. I was getting to know this place all over again. And, after the scorching heat of Arizona, my bones had to get used to the bitter cold that seeped through coats and gloves and hats and settled in the marrow of your bones. I was comparing the wide open spaces of the northwestern plains with the wide open spaces in the southwestern deserts. I looked across the endless pasture of Paul Terrell's ranch that seemed to stop with a screech of brakes at the Rockies rising in the distance. And, once again, I gazed with wonder at the mountains, giant-sized pyramids of slate, the peaks disappearing from sight under caps of clouds and berets of snow.

When Jess turned off onto Kaylin Ridge Road, I came out of my daydream, sat up, and looked at him.

"You're not going to the diner first?" I asked.

He shook his head.

"Figured you might want to get situated, rest a little, maybe unpack."

The clock on the dashboard read 12:30.

"It's lunchtime. Probably have a full house . . ." I thought aloud, my mind clicking over automatically to my role as cook on the lunch shift. "Did you make chicken salad? Did I tell you that I add sliced apples to mine now? What about soup? Are they making Reubens? Did you remember to add the steak sauce to the ground beef before you pressed it into patties?" Then I bit my tongue and slowly looked over at Jess.

Jess has the darkest eyes I've ever seen. I read somewhere that black eyes don't exist in humans. Whoever wrote that is wrong. Jess has black eyes as sure as my butt is wide. And they can get blacker, if that's possible, when he's ticked off (and then you just better get the hell out of the way) or when he's amused about something. He'd set his jaw tighter than the vault at Fort Knox. But the corners of his eyes were turned up. He was enjoying himself.

"It's so damn incredible, Juanita. We managed to keep the diner open while you were takin' a spa vacation getting your aura adjusted. Ain't that just the most extraordinary thing? Even managed to fry up some decent eggs and make a sandwich by myself once in a while."

I snorted.

"Yeah, but it's a good thing I came back when I did. 'Cause if you don't start adding my secret ingredients to the recipes, you'll have to close."

He gave me a look that would warm butter then flipped the turn signal.

"You really *aren't* going to the diner first, are you?"

"Not on your life. If I take you over there now, you'll never leave. Somebody will make a phone call, the whole town will show up and, before you know it, you'll be standing knee-deep in pork chop sandwiches."

He was right. But I was disappointed. I wanted to see the folks again, wanted to be around people who really did *eat* food. Not like the tiny half-sized types I had been cooking for who ordered a stack of pancakes with blueberries, ate one blueberry, then said they were full! I wanted to see Mountain dive into three scrambled eggs, a bowl of grits (with butter), four pancakes, and six slices of bacon. I wanted to hear about the new Wal-Mart that the town was up in arms about, the high school band director's divorce, and Mignon's new boyfriend. Not to mention the fact that Horace Patterson's wife was having a baby and . . . I'd missed Paper Moon. It felt good to be back even if it was for a funeral.

When Jess opened the door to the cabin, I heard barking.

"Dracula! The Queen of Sheba is back!"

That darned dog charged toward me like I was breaking in but stopped just short of tackling me. I held up my hand. Before I left after Christmas, I'd started teaching Dracula a few new tricks.

"Don't slobber on me!" I warned him.

Dracula hung his head as if his feelings had been hurt.

"Don't give me that stuff, you know what I'm talking about," I crooned as I scratched him behind the ears. I frowned as I felt around the dog's shoulders. "Dracula, you feel . . . skinny." I stepped back and studied the Rottweiler, who looked up at me with eager brown eyes and a rapidly wagging tail. "Jess! You aren't feeding him enough! He's so skinny!"

"Humph. Juanita, the dog's growing up, that's all, lost that baby fat. I'm exercising him more. And . . ." He poked his head around the doorway from the bedroom and gave me a sneer. "I don't feed him sissy food like you do. Plain old dog chow, that's what he gets."

"Well, Lordy, no wonder," I commented, squeezing Dracula again, then I shrugged off my heavy coat. 'He's starvin' you t'death," I told the dog, lowering my voice so that Jess wouldn't hear. He thinks that I spoil Dracula. What does he know? "Don't you worry 'bout a thing, I'll get you straight." Dog chow for my baby. I fed Dracula a little chow mixed up with . . . well, that was my and Dracula's little secret.

"This week's mail is in the hall, on the sofa table," Jess yelled from the other room.

I was looking out the windows at the snow. It was so quiet-looking, so clean, not even rabbit tracks to break the cake-icing smoothness. It wasn't tinged with gray or dirty like a February snowfall that's stayed longer than a third cousin from Alabama. It was so white that it sparkled in the little beams of sunlight that sneaked through the trees to the forest floor. A stag held up his nose to catch a scent on the wind. He was the "fourteen pointer" that Bobby Smith coveted. But Jess owned this part of the ridge and posted "No Hunting" signs, so the old stag was safe for now.

"Jess, I'll split the meat with you," Bobby had offered. "Juanita can fix up some venison steaks with one of those fancy French sauces that you like to make." *Nice of him to volunteer my services.*

But Jess had turned him down and I was glad about that. Cooking up the father of Bambi didn't appeal to me.

The mail was on the table in a neat pile with a paperweight on top just as Jess had said. Two pieces of paper got my attention right away. One was a telephone message from my son, Randy. Next to Randy's name, Jess had scrawled, "Not urgent." The other was a large white envelope with a return address from the Arcadia Valley Community and Technical College, Food Services Management Department, Mason, Montana. I fingered the envelope. It was thick. And on the front, in bold red letters, there were the words, "Your future begins at AVCTC!"

"I saw the packet from Arcadia Valley," Jess spoke from the doorway. "Are you and Mignon signing up for another painting class?"

"Yep," I lied, gathering up the rest of the mail and the phone messages.

My heart was thumping in my chest the way it always did whenever my children called. They are grown now, past the age where I have to worry about high fevers or fights on the playground. They have graduated to bigger and better things for me to worry about. Randy was paroled a while back and now works as a sous-chef in a restaurant. I am still learning the lingo.

He had patted me on the shoulder as if I was ten years old.

"No, Momma, not 'cook,' 'chef,' " he'd corrected me.

My baby was sautéing, stir-frying, and searing with the best of them. I was as proud as I could be.

My daughter, Bertie, had come a long way, too. She'd gotten away from the couch, the soap operas, and the beer and was now working two jobs. She was taking business courses at Franklin and had decided to be an accountant. Not a bad job for a girl who'd always been able to count up change in her head from the time she was six and memorize all of the numbers on my lotto tickets, including the tickers.

Rashawn was my wild card. He lived on the edge and he liked it that way. Drugs and guns. He knew what he wanted wasn't anything that I was talking about.

"I'm a businessman, Momma," he would tell me in his cool tenor. It was a voice smooth enough to sing in a church choir. It was a voice that was scalpel sharp when it told you that your time was up and hand over the money. "Every business has its rewards and its risks."

It sounded very black and white, like he was talking about running a dry cleaners or a Starbucks or something. I wished he was making lattes.

"I can take care of myself," Rashawn always said. I had no choice but to believe him but it didn't stop my stomach from churning whenever I got a message from "back home."

"Sixes and Sevens, may I help you?" The female voice was perky. Yep, that's the word. Perky.

"May I speak with Randy Jackson?"

"Chef is out right now," the voice replied. "May I take a message, please?"

"Oh. I'm his mother and I am returning his call."

"Mrs. Louis? Chef Jackson was expecting your call . . . he said to tell you that . . ." I heard the sound of paper rustling. "Here it is. It isn't an emergency, that he and Roberta are fine and he'll call you tomorrow."

Chef Jackson, my, my, we have come up in the world. And has folks taking messages for him, too. I am impressed.

I told her that was fine and hung up. I smiled to myself. I had almost forgotten that my daughter's real name was Roberta.

"Juanita?"

Jess and Dracula stood in the doorway.

"I guess I wasn't thinkin'," he said. "Brought you straight over here without even asking if you'd rather go to Millie's."

I had thought about it. But there would be time for that later.

"What time do you have to be at the diner?"

Jess sent the dog to the front room. His eyes twinkled as he smiled.

"Mental health day," he said simply, pulling me into his arms.

I snorted as I nuzzled his cheek.

"Mental health day, my behind," I told him.

"Exactly what I wanted to talk to you about," Jess murmured as he gave me a squeeze.

I have just one thing to say about Millie Tilson's funeral. I have never seen *anything* like it. And that is saying something 'cause black folks can *do* some funerals.

Number one, we're not in any hurry to get the loved one buried so we have lots of time to plan a spectacle. God forbid that any fourth cousin from Bedbug, Georgia, should miss it! Aunt Sue is coming from Alabama on the Greyhound and won't be here until next week? We'll wait! Cousin Earl's still recovering from gall bladder surgery? Friday after next is fine. The dead will *still* be dead then, won't they? Time is not a factor. If you want to really insult a black undertaker just tell him that you want your loved one's funeral—from the wake to the planting—done in three days. He'll look at you like you've just smacked his momma.

It takes time to coordinate all those details. Gospel choir or senior choir? Will Miss Virginia sing the solo or Sister OraLee? Brother Joseph is playing the organ? What about Mrs. Perkins, the piano teacher? But those are relatively minor issues. If the son of the deceased wants Reverend Smith to deliver the eulogy and the daughter wants Father Jones, you have a problem that might take a few more days to iron out. You have to decide whether the service will be held at Second Street AME or Mount Ararat

Baptist! And if you have a Methodist issue or if there's an Episcopalian convert, forget about it. You might end up putting your loved one on ice because the family will argue about that mess until Kingdom come. Last but definitely not least, there is the decision of which funeral home to use.

This issue alone has been known to bring about divorce, incite violence, and create rifts between folks wider than the Mississippi River. In a community of any size, there are at least two black funeral homes. Half of the folks in town use one (and have since Moses was a boy), the other half uses the other one. There are usually members of both camps in one family.

"I wouldn't send a dead mouse to Robertson's," says the brother-in-law. The fight begins there. Voices rise, threats are made, and tears shed. The arguing only ends when someone (once again, it's usually an in-law) suggests cremation. The guns may come out then. You know black folks have to have a body to cry over, and we love wakes. They are the next best thing to wedding receptions.

When it's all said and done, you don't have a funeral, you have an event (or an ordeal, depending on your point of view) with music, testimonials, preaching, crying (I'm not talkin' about delicate sniffles into cloth handkerchiefs either, I'm talkin' about gut-wrenching sobs, "Lord, Jesus, help me!"s, and mounds of wadded-up Kleenex), and little "side" services from this guild, that club, or fraternity or sorority. Bring your lunch because you'll be there all day. There will be food served afterward but you'll need a snack to get you through the three-hour service.

Before Millie's going-home, that was my experience with funerals. But this was Silver Lake County, Montana, settled by Presbyterian Scots, Lutheran Germans and Swedes, with a few free-range Baptists and Methodists thrown in for flavoring. When Millie went to church, which wasn't often, she attended First Presbyterian in Mason. So I had prepared myself for a forty-five-minute one-hymn-two-prayer-reading-of-the-obituary-dust-to-dust-ashes-to-ashes-it's-11:45-let's-wrap-this-up service with coffee and cake afterward to fortify the family.

Man, was I wrong.

The folks at First Presbyterian were not ready. And neither was I.

I wore a black sweater and matching long skirt—an appropriate "going to a meeting" outfit. Looking back on it, I should have worn a cocktail dress and heels.

Millie had written instructions for her funeral. She had outlined in detail the music, flowers, reception hall, type of champagne, hors d'oeuvres, and the location of that Maine bocker suit she'd wanted to be buried in. Millie didn't leave anything to chance.

She had an accomplice. Reverend Hare had grown up on the farm next to the Tilsons, having lived with them for a while when he was a boy after his mother died. Millie was like his big sister. He did anything she told him to. And that included having a jazz trio soothe the mourners instead of the pipe organ, testimonials from Millie's friends, including a Texas oilman and a few retired Follies Bergere chorus girls, and the recorded strains of The Preservation Hall Band playing "When the Saints Go Marching In" as the casket was carried from the church. There were some gasps when a heavily made-up and obviously male, but dressed as a female, soloist gave a moving rendition of "You'll Never Walk Alone" but, other than that, I thought the residents of Mason, Paper Moon, and other parts of Lake, Silver Lake, Mineral, and Missoula counties in south-western Montana coped pretty well with the unorthodox service. They listened quietly to the sermons—all three of them—given by (in order) a Buddhist priest, a female Druid (if I'm lyin', I'm flyin'), and the accommodating Reverend Thomas Hare, on behalf of the Presbyterians. Later, the Reverend confided that he'd had one of the Altar Guild ladies standing by with smelling salts, water, and pillows in case any of the mourners were overcome.

After the service, the mourners were invited to pay their respects to the family and bring their dancing shoes. That's what it said at the bottom of the program. *"Bring your dancing shoes."* In my experience, postfuneral activity means fried chicken in the church basement or church-lady lasagna at the family home. I should have known that Millie Tilson would not have anything as boring as that. Folks were invited to pay their respects at the Mason Ramada Inn. And it was not a quiet, solemn pat-the-family-on-the-back-and-we'll-keep-you-in-our-prayers affair. It was a cabaret.

There were at least a hundred fifty people there, maybe more. Millie had contacted the motel's manager in advance (his grandmother was one of her bridge partners) so when he found out about her passing, he knew just what he was supposed to do.

Jess and I stood in the corner like two wallflowers sipping our Dom Perignon (slowly, because we knew how much it cost) and trying not to stare too hard at Millie's friends, both Montanans and "others," dancing around the room in a conga line. There was a live band, champagne, and hors d'oeuvres trucked in from a la-di-da place in Missoula. (California rolls and smoked salmon were not on the banquet menu of the Mason Ramada.) Not only were the townsfolk of Paper Moon in attendance (the whole town closed down to go to Millie's funeral) but the colorful members of Millie's past lives (and she'd had many) were also there. The parade of characters made cable television seem stale.

The six-foot-three-inch transvestite soloist came with three similarly dressed colleagues from Miami's South Beach. They'd known Millie when she'd owned a condo there.

"Girl," gushed Patsy Pinkman, a nearly seven-foot-tall wonder who could salsa in high heels better than I walked in sneakers and who had once played men's college basketball, "Millie gave the best partays. Champagne fountains, tables groaning with food, great music, and the cutest waiters . . ." He batted his inch-long eyelashes at me. "I'll miss the old girl. Here's to her!" He lifted the squatty little glass of neat bourbon and dropped it with one gulp.

"Takes a real man to do that," Jess observed solemnly. Together, we watched Patsy P, as she, er, he, liked to be called, move to the center of the floor and start an electric-slide line. Reverend Hare and Mr. and Mrs. Olson joined them.

A whole plane of Texans had come up from Austin and San Antonio, business colleagues of Millie's last husband, the oilman Paul Daniels. They did the Texas two-step to Bootsy Collins in their ostrich and alligator cowboy boots. The staff of Francine's Beauty World—from Francine with her platinum blonde twelve-inch-high beehive to the shampoo girl with fuchsia-colored tresses—came, bringing their dates. Even the members of Millie's creative writ-

ing class at the college stopped by. These were mostly college kids wearing black (but not for mourning) with studs
in their noses and ears. They congregated together in the
corners of the ballroom looking like latter-day vampires,
waiting for the food train to arrive and only becoming an-
imated when someone put on (by mistake) a heavy-metal
CD. It was quite a bunch.

I two-stepped with a man named "Bud" for a little while
and tried to keep up with the electric slide without getting
trampled but had to give up the floor when the showgirls
joined us. We'd started doing "the Bump" and, with my
wide hips, I was afraid that I'd bump into one of them and
break a bone—my bones, not theirs.

The retirement home of former Follies Bergere dancers
was well represented by ten ladies who claimed to have
been in the chorus line with Millie back in the twirties.
When I asked what that meant, one of them (a striking
woman with navel orange–colored hair) cackled, "Darling,
we can't remember if we danced with her in the twenties or
in the thirties, so we just put the two together."

"Barbara," one of the other ladies chimed in. "It might
have been the forties!"

They made quite a sight.

Now, Jess is rarely impressed or surprised by anything.
But the sight of these old ladies moving around the dance-
floor ballroom of the Mason Ramada was more than he
was ready for. They danced with canes and without. Some
of them wore sneakers, some of them wore forties-style
platform heels. One thing they had in common, though. I
have more gray in my head than any of them had in theirs.

"These old bats better be careful, they'll break a hip!" he
exclaimed as one of them twirled by in the arms of one of

the "boys" from South Beach. Both she and *he* were wearing platform shoes.

"Watch your language," I shouted back to him. The music was really loud. "Not 'old,' 'mature.' "

"Mature, hell," snorted Jess, watching one of the brightly rouged octogenarians scamper across the floor doing the salsa with a walker. Now, that was a sight. "These women are *artifacts!*"

Mountain stomped by with his girlfriend on his arm, moving like a tree stump with legs. He and his girl are cute together but they don't quite fit. For whatever reason, Mountain likes to date the tiniest, skinniest little girls that he can find. "I like to pretend that they're Tinkerbell," he says.

"Mountain, that's sick," Jess tells him.

Mountain is now dating Lawra Swenson, all five feet and ninety-five pounds of her. Watching them dance together is like watching a Saint Bernard cha-cha with a Chihuahua. Mountain looks like he's fighting off a swarm of bees and Lawra looks as if she's dancing with the Jolly White Giant. Very interesting.

"Excuse me!"

I jumped because it was so noisy and the owner of this comment had just yelled in my ear to make sure that I'd hear him.

He was a tall, thin, unassuming man, wearing wire-rim eyeglasses and a business suit. He had perfectly cut light brown-colored hair and watery blue eyes. He looked like a lawyer.

He handed me his business card. He *was* a lawyer.

"You're Juanita Louis, aren't you?"

"Yes, I am!" I yelled back.

"I want to introduce myself," he said very slowly and loudly, "I'm Geoff Black. I'm Mrs. Daniels's attorney."

"Mrs. Who?"

"Mrs. Daniels. Sorry, Miss Tilson. She hired me when she was Mrs. Paul Hillman Daniels." *Right, the oil man.*

"Oh," I answered. "Nice to meet you." It was funny thinking of Millie as a "Mrs." Anybody. She had always just been Millie Tilson, even though everyone knew that she'd been through more husbands than there were holidays in a year.

"I need to confirm your mailing address," he yelled.

The band had been playing "Super Freak" and the fossilized chorus girls, the boys from South Beach, and the Mason City council were on the dance floor.

"My what?" I thought I heard him say that he liked my dress.

"Your mailing address," he repeated, moving closer to my ear. "Box 4, Rural Route 17, Paper Moon, Montana?"

"That's the diner but that's OK, I'll get it," I told him. "What are you sending?"

"You are listed as a beneficiary in Mrs., um, Ms. Tilson's will. Each beneficiary has to be notified pursuant to probate law." He said this as if to make himself seem more lawyerly or something. It helped because the last time I saw him, he was dancing but looked as if he had ten-ton boulders on his feet.

"Oh. OK," I said because I couldn't think of anything else to say.

"I'll be in touch because—" Mr. Black started to say something else but was interrupted by the deejay's announcement that the conga line was forming at the opposite end of the room. One of the mummified showgirls grabbed him by the arm and pushed him in that direction. He waved back at me with an apologetic expression. The showgirl gave me a wink of one heavily mascaraed eye.

"He's got a cute ass," she yelled over her shoulder.

On the way back to Paper Moon, it suddenly came to me what the attorney had said.

Jess thought that the whole thing was funny.

"Got the old woman to write you into her will, huh?"

"She probably just left me her old movie collection. Or her shoes. We wear the same size."

Jess made a face as he turned the corner.

"You don't want her shoes."

"No, I don't . . ." I murmured, looking at the night sky. I couldn't fill Millie's shoes. I wished she'd left me her spirit and her nerve. I wish she'd left me the strength to say "I can" instead of "I can't." I was thinking about the white envelope from the community college that I hadn't opened yet—the one that might hold my future inside. I was thinking about my last conversation with Nina, about being her business partner.

"I didn't like Will Rogers as much as other folks did," Millie had said once while she was working on her laptop, her glasses perched on her nose, her fingers flying. "But that man did have a few wise things to say. Said once that even if you're on the right track, you'll get run over if you just sit there."

It's true.

I looked across the highway toward the street where Millie's house sat near the top of the hill. The old place would always be "Millie's House," no matter who lived there, no matter what happened to it. It was dusk and the house was lit up, including the Tower Room, Elva Van Roan's third-floor domain.

Yeah. She'd probably just left me her old movie collection.

Chapter Six

Just when life gets hectic and overwhelming, some pious soul will say, in a back-of-the-church whisper, "God never gives us more than we can handle." They don't know what they're talking about. Here's the gospel according to Juanita: Sometimes, God sneaks a quick one in just to see how much we can take before our legs buckle. It's a test. But it's hard to know, when it's all over, whether you've passed or not. That comes later.

That's the way I felt about my homecoming to Paper Moon. It was bad enough that I came back because there was a death in the family, so to speak. But from Millie's funeral on, it was just one damn thing after another. My great adventure began to stall like a '78 Oldsmobile Deuce and a quarter left out in the cold too long.

The Thursday after Millie's farewell party, I couldn't sleep so I got up before the sun. Jess stuck his nose out from under the covers.

"Juanita, Randolph starts the breakfast run on Thursday mornings. The diner's covered, you don't have to go in."

I pulled the blanket back over his head.

"So, I'll help. I'm up, I might as well do something," I told him. It was as if I had real ants in my pants— I couldn't sleep, I couldn't sit still. I showed up at the diner at six o'clock in the morning just as I used to do, was tackled by Dracula, had to change the station on the radio (I think Mountain tuned it to "easy listening" on purpose), and found the breakfast supplies laid out for me as if I was an executive chef. It was a good thing that some of the snow had melted, though, or I would have slid all the way down Kaylin's Ridge Road. Randolph, another one of Jess's young cousins, and I worked side by side to get things ready. Fish, Abel, and the boys stomped through the door at six-forty-five sharp, even though it wasn't fishing weather, knocking the snow off their boots and making a ruckus as usual. They didn't seem surprised to see me behind the counter.

Fish spat a wad of tobacco into the spittoon and gave me a wave.

Abel said, "How you doing, Juanita?" like he saw me every day and life picked up from there.

Sort of.

That next Saturday, the furnace went out and even though we shut down for dinner (you can't eat gourmet food if you're freezin' to death), I still cooked breakfast that morning for a dining room full of people! (It was a little chilly, but this is Montana.) Jess built a huge fire in the stone fireplace and I cooked up eggs, sausage, and my new Sedona Southwest Omelet like I was Frontier Sallie. Shoot, my great-grandparents sharecropped in Georgia. You think they had central heating? Then, we had a heat wave. The sun came out; the outside thermometer read fifty-five degrees, and most of the snow melted. Some of those fools were walking around without coats. The creek flooded and River Walk Road was closed. Apparently, Mother Nature has hot flashes, too.

But it was too good to last. A front came in from Alaska. The temperature dropped like a stone in the bathtub. And so did everything else. I remembered something my mother had said: "If it weren't for bad luck, we wouldn't have any luck at all!"

"Momma, I'm not sure how to tell you this," Randy said slowly over the telephone.

Oh, Lordy, I was ready to find a nice, dark closet, walk in, and lock the door.

Rashawn had been arrested for drug trafficking and his case was going to a grand jury. I took a deep breath and closed my eyes. Well, I guess it could have been worse. Whenever I get a phone call about that boy, I'm scared they're going to tell me he's been shot or worse.

"How did you find out?" I asked. Rashawn didn't call me anymore when he got picked up. We'd had that conversation. I had told him not to call me to put up bail, get him out, or any other such stuff. It had gotten to be too much of a habit.

"Saw him yesterday, he came by for lunch," Randy answered.

Came by for lunch? That was a picture that I wanted to see: Rashawn sitting at a little bistro table, munching on a Caesar salad, drinking sparkling water.

"He's doing well?" I couldn't think of anything else to say. I'm sure the owner of Sixes and Sevens was just tickled to have a nearly indicted drug dealer in his place.

Randy snorted and, at first, I thought that he was laughing. But when he spoke again, I heard the bitterness in his voice.

"Oh, yes, ma'am," he answered. "He's real proud of himself, says he'll beat this thing. He has the most expensive lawyer in town, some guy named Harrison, and posted bail faster than you could say . . . shoot. He must have some pretty good . . . contacts."

"Moving up in the world," I said, more to myself than to Randy. I guess the days of calling me at 3:00 AM asking for two hundred dollars were long gone. Rashawn was in the big leagues now and leaving the little people behind.

"Didn't mean to spoil your day, Momma," Randy apologized. "Just thought you'd want to know."

I knew that Randy meant well but I wasn't sure I did want to know. Rashawn moves in a dimension that I do not want to visit.

The thirty-degree drop in temperature froze the pipes in the diner and left us with a mess in the basement and a very happy plumber.

But the phone still worked.

"Momma!" Now, it was Bertie. I held my breath. My daughter was doing OK, much better than when I left, but, like Rashawn, I only heard from her secondhand through Randy. She didn't call me directly unless she wanted something real bad. After about twenty seconds of small talk, I could tell that she couldn't stand it anymore. She was ready to plunge in. "I was wondering . . . could you come home and keep Teishia for me? Just for spring quarter?"

Just for spring quarter? Oh, is that all?

I felt my hair turning white before I could answer. The last time Bertie left Teishia with me "just for" a certain unspecified period of time, she was gone for four days and I never even got a phone call. I loved T but, let's face it, I have done children. Hadn't planned on doing much more with the grandbabies than hug 'em, buy 'em toys, and hand 'em back. And what made Bertie think I wanted to "come home"?

"Bertie, I hadn't planned on coming back to Ohio . . . anytime soon."

"Oh, then I could bring her out there," she answered without missing a beat. *Bless her heart, this is not a girl to take no for an answer. She always has a backup plan.*

You'd better think again, I said to myself.

"No, Bertie, I don't think so," I told her. The last time I made arrangements for a babysitter, Ronald Reagan was president. Or was it Jimmy Carter?

My daughter was not to be put off by my hesitation, the fact that I had my own life, or that I said, "No." This is a gal who will definitely run a corporation someday. She has no compunctions about running over anybody. She went on with the conversation like I hadn't said anything at all.

"Can you let me know by the fifteenth, so I can make my plans?" *Her plans?*

Every damn thing at once, I said to myself, my stomach tying itself into a knot.

By the time I got off the telephone, Jess had the plumbing estimate so we were both in a bad mood. The damage was bad and, what was even worse, it would take a couple of days to fix so the diner had to remain closed. Jess was in the growling stage and I wasn't too far behind him.

Then the mailman showed up with a certified letter. For me.

"It's from the attorney, Geoff Black, the guy I met at the

funeral," I reminded him, reading off the four names on the letterhead. "Remember? He said that I was a beneficiary."

"Prob'bly left you the damn cats," Jess grumbled from behind the counter, turning off the lights as he locked up. Jess hates cats.

My mood wasn't any better than his. Rashawn in trouble again. Bertie making plans to drop a three-year-old in my lap. All the new possibilities dissolved. My old life was chasing me and I couldn't run fast enough. I wondered what else I would have to deal with.

"Or else she left me the damn ghost," I murmured.

It was worse than that.

Millie had left me the B&B: house, cats, ghost, *everything*. This is the part in the romance novel where the heroine faints. I would have, too, if I'd known how.

Since I was too stunned to faint, I just sat in the chair in attorney Geoff Black's office with my eyes bugged out and my mouth hanging open. My brain wasn't working so the words I'd started to say wouldn't come out of my mouth. I was so surprised at what the attorney had said, I inhaled but didn't exhale. I must have looked as if I was about to go into shock.

"Ms. Louis, are you all right?" Geoff Black leaned forward with a worried expression on his face. "Do you need a glass of water?"

"Juanita, you OK?" Jess patted me on the arm.

I was staring at Mr. Black.

"She left me the whole house?" I asked. A stupid question. What did I think, that Millie was going to leave me the first floor and leave the rest to somebody else?

Geoff smiled slightly.

"Yes, the whole house and a small annuity for upkeep.

Mrs. Daniels, er, Miss Tilson said that old houses are like old showgirls. They need maintenance every once in a while."

That certainly was something Millie would have said, all right. But, why me?

"What about her family?" I asked. I thought about her sister and Horace and her other nieces and nephews. Geoff shook his head and glanced down at the paper.

"She's left them some very generous bequests. They won't have any complaints. Miss Tilson was a wealthy woman. But she felt that you would be the perfect person to carry on her legacy."

Me? Millie's legacy? With the tentacles from my past life reaching out to pull me back? What was she thinking?

"Congratulations, Miz Louis," Jess said. "You got yourself a business."

His eyes danced with merriment and he smiled.

Ask and ye shall receive.

Well, I'd been thinking about running a business. A bed-and-breakfast business. Now, I had one right in my lap.

Geoff Black's cough brought me out of my daydream.

"I would hold on the congratulations for the moment," he said. I could hear thunderclouds in his voice. He fumbled with the papers in his hands. "I'm not sure how to say this, Ms. Louis, but . . . well, there may be a slight impediment to the bequest. Nothing to really worry about." He paused. "I don't think."

"Slight" was not the word I would have used to describe the "impediment."

"The will has been contested. A hearing hasn't been set yet but I expect the papers to be filed soon and then Judge McGriff will set a date."

"By who?"

"I'll handle the will contest hearing," Geoff went on, not answering my question. "The complainant alleges that Miss Tilson was not of sound mind when she made her will and that all bequests are void. If that happens, the estate reverts to the heirs as dictated by probate law when a person dies intestate." He paused for a moment. "Because of Millie's, well, eccentric behavior . . . it could be a challenging case."

Ask a lawyer where he's going, he'll tell you where he's been.

"Who's contesting the will?"

"Oh, sorry. In this case, it's pretty simple. It means that Miss Tilson's entire estate would go to one person. Her son."

"Her son?" Jess and I answered in a duet.

The lawyer smiled sheepishly.

"I get that a lot," he said. "It isn't really common knowledge that Millie had a son, even in Paper Moon where everybody knows everybody's business or *thinks* that they know everybody's business. But Millie did have her secrets and, unlike most folks around here, she was pretty good at keeping them. I've handled her legal affairs for some time but . . . well, attorney-client privilege being what it is . . ."

"Who is . . . where is . . . was he born in Montana?" I was recovering from the shock. But I wasn't too shocked to be nosy. "Or is that information privileged?" I asked, using his word.

Geoff shrugged his shoulders.

"Not anymore. At least half the town should know by now. Her son was born in Kenya, brought up in the UK, educated in the UK and the United States. He's very wealthy, like the old-time tycoons. It's quite a story."

And then I remembered that I had heard at least part of it—a story that Millie told me one summer night when the sky was so dark and clear that you could see the stars back to forever; a love story about a dancer and a wealthy farmer, set in Kenya. But was it a story—a short story that she had told me was for her creative writing class at the UM Extension—or was it true? Now, the words were coming back to me and I remembered the faraway look in Millie's eyes when she spoke them. I remembered the purring of Asim, the Siamese cat who she'd held in her lap.

She knew that, while it was easy to stay in paradise, it was better, even braver perhaps, to leave. She still had mountains of her own to climb. Even though she left everything she ever loved in his hands.

What she'd left in his hands was her baby. Her story wasn't make-believe at all. Dear Millie.

"So, what do I do now?" I asked. I felt as if someone had given me a birthday present, changed their mind, and taken it back, wrapping paper, tape, bow, and all.

"Until the hearing, which will probably take place in six weeks, the will stands, as written . . . more or less," Geoff added uncertainly.

That wasn't helpful. I felt a stone settle in my stomach.

"Oh, and you might want to get involved with the inn," Geoff answered, closing his file folder. "During the interim."

I wanted to melt into a puddle and just drip away.

"What about . . . the son? What's his name?"

"Broderick Tilson Hayward-Smith," Geoff answered. "Oh, I forgot to tell you. Mr. Hayward-Smith is flying in, sometime before the hearing. He wants to stay at the inn, get a feel for the place." Geoff looked at me sympathetically. "I guess he's checking out what he hopes will be his inheritance." Then Geoff frowned. "Although his attorneys say that he'd like to tear down the place and sell the land to the VFW for a parking lot."

Six weeks? This man was coming in six weeks to stay at the inn? And the lawyer forgot to tell me?

The phone rang just in time to keep me from crawling over that desk and smacking Geoff Black in the head with a stack of file folders.

"Hello?" He listened for a moment then looked up at me. "It's for you."

It was Inez and her girdle was in a knot. She needed help and could I stop by? The inn would be full of guests by the weekend with reservations booked last year. There was a list of unreturned phone calls and food to order. Millie's house had been closed for most of the winter. FedEx had delivered four boxes—of something—and the carpet cleaners were coming on Wednesday. There was a stack of unopened mail, unpaid bills, and one of the cats had disappeared again. She didn't have to tell me which one.

I grumbled, growled, and just plain bitched all the way back to Paper Moon.

"I thought God didn't give you more than you could handle," I complained to Jess. "What did I do to deserve all this?"

Jess did not feel sorry for me.

"Quit complaining!" he shot back. "You're smart, hardworking, a halfway decent cook." He winked at me. "You're a little contrary but I still love you. And you're more resourceful than most foxes I've seen."

I guess that's a compliment.

"But I don't know anything about business and accounting and reservations and . . . besides, I've already . . ." I shut my mouth. Nina's quirky face appeared. The thick white envelope from Arcadia Valley Community and Technical College was still unopened. And there was Bertie.

"Juanita, you just concentrate on keeping that inn from going under until after the probate hearing. Then you can sit back and decide just what you're going to do in the long run."

"What kind of people would take a vacation in Montana in the winter? This is stupid!"

"No, this is business," Jess barked out. "Folks don't wait on the weather to break as much as they used to. Millie saw the trend and rode the wave. Smart old lady."

"Crazy old lady," I said.

"Don't say that to anyone else," Jess warned. "If the probate judge agrees with you, you're out of an inheritance."

By the end of that week, sitting by Nina's pool in Sedona doing nothing was beginning to look real good.

Millie's was a crazy house.

Inez was so upset that half of her sentences were in English and the other half were in Spanish. The "to do" list was longer than a giraffe's neck. Millie had been sick a long time and things had just been left to take care of themselves.

The refrigerators hadn't been stocked in a while, the parlor furniture had a half inch of dust on it, and the bedrooms needed to be aired out. There were stacks of unopened mail, newspapers, and magazines from as far back as Christmas, and twenty telephone messages to return. Millie's e-mail box was "full," whatever that meant, and . . . did I mention the half inch of dust in the parlor?

I wanted to scream. I wanted to run back out the door and down the road to the diner and lock myself in the pantry. I wanted to tell God, or whoever else was listening, that I was grateful for the gift but that it had been given to the wrong woman. I couldn't do this. I am not a businesswoman. I didn't have what it took. I didn't know how.

I stood in the doorway of Millie's suite. I hadn't been here since my last visit to Paper Moon over the holidays. Everything was the same except for the empty space in the middle of her bedroom where the hospital bed had been. I walked around the room and could smell a faint thread of fragrance, the Secret of Venus perfume that Millie wore. Books were stacked on top of her nightstands and her tortoiseshell-tipped cigarette holder was perched on the delicate bone-china ashtray. And, on top of the delicate lady's desk, which sat in the corner in front of the tower window, were her laptop and her files. Like a quiet spirit, Millie was in every corner of this room. It kind of got to me and, for a moment, I just stood there, frozen, with just my memories of her in my head. Suddenly, I heard bumping on the third floor above, probably Inez running the sweeper, and remembered that I was supposed to be organizing, cleaning, and managing, whatever that meant—not crying.

I wiped the tears from my eyes and headed toward the door. I went down the back staircase. What would Millie have done first? Make a list. She always said that no project was too difficult to put down on paper. The rest of it, I would have to worry about later.

Inez and I worked like fiends, there is no other way to say it. We called in Gwen, who sometimes worked at the inn, and we all worked hard for the next three days to get the place ready for its weekend guests *and* for Broderick

Tilson Hayward-Smith. I didn't cook during that time. Instead, I called out for pizza or gobbled down the meals that Jess sent over from the diner, including a tuna-salad sandwich that he made. He had remembered to put in a pinch of sugar.

"Everything has got to be perfect," I told Inez later for the three hundredth time. "Millie's son will stay here for the hearing. I want everything just right."

Inez frowned.

"Then maybe we should make it not so perfect," she commented. I could hear the anger in her voice. "Then he will not want it so much." Inez was furious at the thought of Mr. Hayward-Smith turning the B&B into part of the parking lot for the VFW.

Actually, that wasn't such a bad idea. The house needed some work and it was really old. But I knew how Millie felt about this place. Regardless of the circumstances, she would be furious if the inn were in less than A-plus shape. When Millie was alive, there was never any dust, the carpets were vacuumed two times a day, and the rooms always had fresh flowers in them. I couldn't do any less than that. Especially since it was Millie's son who would be our most important guest. Inez headed for the second floor to check out the Violet Room one last time. Gwen was dusting the demitasse cups in the huge china cabinet in the dining room. I grabbed the silver service and headed toward the kitchen. I would polish it until it was brighter than a searchlight.

Later, I walked back to the little office that was behind the kitchen to pick up papers that Inez had set out for me. Above, on the second floor, I heard a door slam. Then, something heavy dropped on the floor. It shook the crystal chandelier in the dining room. Someone with the shoe size of a bull elephant stomped down the hall toward the back of the house and another door slammed. Then the house was quiet again.

I looked up at the ceiling where the chandelier was still swaying.

What on earth was she *doing* up there?

My question was answered when she rushed in from the front porch with the day's mail. The cold air swirled around me and I shivered. Inez stomped her feet and quickly closed the door, rubbing her shoulders.

"Here is today's mail, I . . . what is wrong?" she asked. I must have looked as if I'd seen . . .

"Is Gwen still here? Or Bea?" I asked, hopefully, even though I thought that I already knew the answer.

Inez shook her head and sorted through the mail.

"No, she left at five. Bea comes in tomorrow. ¿Por qué?"

"Oh. OK," I said slowly. "Then we have a problem," I added, looking up at the crown-molded ceiling. There were scraping noises coming from the Mauve Room just above us. It was as if a chair was being dragged across the wood floor.

We listened for a second, then I looked at Inez. I was hoping that she would tell me that her niece was helping out today. Inez read my expression, then sighed.

"Oh. Sí. I forgot to tell you . . ."

How many times was I going to hear *that*?

"Ever since Millie die, well, Elva, she is not happy. She locks herself in the bathroom. She stomps down the hall, slams doors. Moves the furniture here, moves the furniture there. I don't know *what* to do. Last time she had a tantrum, Millie call a ghost therapist but I can't find the woman's card."

Ghost therapist? You've got to be kidding.

"So, now, I have a ghost with . . . issues?" I asked. This was more than I wanted to deal with. OK, the inn was haunted. It was just something I'd had to accept while I stayed with Millie. I'll admit it, I don't do ghosts. I feel about them almost the way I feel about spiders. If there is a spider in the room, I'll leave the room to the spider. Can't stand the creepy things. Same with ghosts. But most of the time, Elva was cool, kept to herself, and didn't bother anyone. There wasn't any howling or walking through doors. She didn't wake you up in the middle of the night or bring her friends along from the other side to entertain. She minded her own business, whatever that was, and I minded mine.

And now, *she* was upset?

We had guests coming in less than twenty-four hours. And in that time, I had to put out towels; polish the brass door knockers one last time; fluff the quilts, pillows, and comforters; dust the chandeliers; mail the invoices to the lawyer's office; make sure that Lowell's Towing Service shoveled the walks and the driveway if it snowed again; and a million other things.

The last damn thing I needed was a ghost with personal problems.

I took the stairs two steps at a time and marched down the hall to the back staircase that led to the Tower Suite. I opened the door and looked up. The door at the top of the landing was open and I could see the floral wallpaper that bordered the ceiling in the tiny sitting room.

I started to go up but I am not a total fool. I've seen Elva Van Roan before. But, unlike some things in life, once was enough. I am quite happy to talk to her without seeing through her.

So I stayed at the bottom of the stairs.

"Elva, I know you're up there. I hear you knocking and bumping around. Now listen here. I know you're upset that Millie's gone. *You could go with her, you know,*" I added under my breath. Do ghosts hear well? "Now, I'm trying to manage this place and keep everything together if I can. But I'm gonna need some help. We've got guests coming tomorrow and Millie's son will be here pretty soon. Now if things don't go well . . . and if you get to charging around and slamming things and dropping stuff and just plain making a damn fool of yourself . . . well, all I got to say is, if this hearing doesn't go my way, you may be a homeless ghost trying to find an empty plot at Glen Rest, 'cause the attorney says that Mr. Hayward-Smith wants to tear down this place and turn it into a parking lot."

I stopped for a minute. The house was quiet. Inez and I looked at each other.

"You got to give me a break, Elva. We all miss Millie. But you knew her. We have to get on with it." I paused. "Do we have a deal or not?"

I heard Inez exhale loudly. I shrugged my shoulders and turned to go back downstairs.

Then the door at the top of the third-floor landing slammed shut. But there weren't any sounds after that.

Inez's eyes were huge.

So were mine.

"I'll take that as a 'yes,'" I said loudly.

Chapter Seven

I never thought I'd say this (and I'll deny it to my dyin' day) but I'm starting to look back on my Sedona days and wonder if I shouldn't have paid more attention to all that restoring your soul and quieting-the-mind stuff. Maybe I should have taken the yoga class that Nina told me about, stood on my head for a few hours. Or hiked into the canyon to attend a healing meditation. There were hot rock massages that I passed up and Om sessions to help me clean out my mental toxins. And I could have had a spirit dusting for twenty percent off!

Why didn't I do those things? Instead, I chuckled at all the metaphysical talk and avoided the vortex guides like I was running away from food poisoning. By the end of my first month back in Paper Moon, I was ready to pack up and run away. Again.

Inez dropped me off at Jess's cabin one Thursday night. The inn had reopened without a problem (amazing) and weekend guests were coming that Friday. We had worked like crazy women to get the B&B back to its old self and had pretty much succeeded. Even Elva Van Roan had been helpful—no public appearances and she hadn't moved any of the furniture. It was after ten and Jess looked up when I came in. He turned down the sound on the basketball game. I struggled to get out of my coat and hat and boots. I felt as if I was a hundred years old with arthritis, rheumatism, sciatica (What is that, anyway?), and dropsy—all together.

He didn't seem to be surprised to see me. I had been staying at Millie's off and on, half of my stuff was there, half of my stuff was here, and then there were some boxes that Randy had sent from Columbus that were sitting, unopened, in Jess's second bedroom. I was like an itinerant preacher, leaving bits and pieces of myself all over the place. But tonight, I had to get out of Millie's. Besides, the Mauve Room had been reserved for the weekend.

"You look like death warmed over," he commented, setting down his glasses and coming over to help me as I fumbled with my coat.

"Thanks for the compliment," I said.

"You feeling OK?" he asked as he hung up my coat in the closet.

"I feel like shit," I told him. I was so tired that I couldn't think of a better word.

He kissed me gently on the cheek and took my hand.

"I know how to fix that," he said quietly. He clicked off the TV and led me down the hall.

If my body was fading, my mind was racing. And it raced off into a completely wrong direction. My mouth almost said the wrong thing. I stopped midway down the hall.

"Jess . . . I don't feel like . . . well . . ." I sighed.

Jess gave me one of his signature "you-are-a-silly-woman" looks and opened the door to the bathroom instead of the bedroom.

"No kidding. And here I thought that a hot bath worked for almost anybody."

All I could do was bite my lower lip and wrap my arms around his neck. This man is always doing something to cut me a path through the wilderness.

The tub was full of bubbles and there were candles everywhere, the tiny ladylike ones that smelled like fresh-cut roses and reminded me of spring. The room had a nice yellow glow, soft and quiet. He had laid out two huge towels and a fancy sponge like the ones they used in the spas. My bathrobe was hanging on the door and my slippers had been set right next to the tub so that I could slip my corns into them when I got out. The room was warm and cozy despite the ten-degree temperature outside.

Jess cleared his throat.

"Good thing you came when you did or the water would be cold." He spoke with a completely stony expression but, as usual, his eyes were laughing at me.

"How did you . . ."

"Inez phoned just before you left. Take off your clothes. That's an order."

The water was hot (just the way I like it), the bubbles were everywhere (on me, on Jess, on the floor), and I closed my eyes and leaned back against the pillow that Jess put under my head. Perfect.

"This is nice. How'd you learn so much about spa stuff?" I asked him.

"Asked Nina to send me the works," he answered as he

gently washed my arms with the sponge. "I'm gonna give you a bath, then a pedicure."

I opened one eye and gave him a doubtful look. A pedicure?

"Wash there, no, *there*," I directed him between sighs.

"I'm not washing," he growled. "I'm exfoliating."

Washing, exfoliating, fondling, whatever.

"You're just doing this to get cheap feels," I told him. I sighed again. Then I smiled as his hands reached a certain spot. "Could you feel there again, please?"

He chuckled and did what I asked.

By the time he worked his way down to my feet, I was so relaxed that Jess had to keep poking me so that I would stay awake. He washed my feet, then each toe one by one, bunions, corns, calluses, and all. It tickled.

"I really needed this," I managed to murmur. "I'm worn out. Crash and burn . . ." I probably didn't make any sense at all.

Jess turned on the tap and ran more hot water into the tub.

"That ain't no surprise. You just got back, went to a funeral, found out you're an heiress, and now you're working more hours than a West Virginia coal miner."

I opened one eye.

"Now what would a Montana boy know about West Virginia coal miners?"

He began to massage my feet.

"I get around."

"Ummm . . ."

"You've been opening up the diner, *after* I told you not to, working at the inn, and you jump every time the phone rings."

I closed the one eye that I had opened.

"And I wasn't going to mention this, but . . ." Jess kissed the bottom of my right foot. "There's a thick white envelope from Arcadia Valley that's been setting around collectin' dust. If I were the curious type, which I'm not, I would have opened it by now. Especially seein' as you haven't. And Nina called."

I didn't say anything.

"What's wrong, Miz Louis?" he asked. "You've been running around here like a chicken with its head cut off. You're hardly sleeping and I might be mistaken but I don't think you're eatin' right, either. I'll have to drop you if you lose that nice derriere of yours." With that comment, he gave me a squeeze and I almost jumped out of the tub.

"Quit it!" I kicked at him. He caught my foot again and kissed it. Oh, I just love that.

"What's got your thong in such a knot?"

"I don't wear thongs," I told him defiantly.

Jess grinned.

"Yeah, I know. Been meanin' to talk with you about *that*, too. But don't change the subject. What's wrong?"

"I'm feelin' a bit . . . like I got too much on my plate." I'd heard that term somewhere. Really didn't like it much but it seemed to fit my situation.

Jess snorted.

"No, woman, you ain't just got too much on your plate. You've got a full set of china and every damn plate, saucer, and bowl is full." He shook his head as he leaned down to grab the sponge that had slipped out of his hand.

I buried my face in the bubbles.

"There's so much . . . that's right. I don't want to bitch about a few little things . . ."

"Juanita . . ."

"OK. There's the inn. There's the diner. There's Bertie . . ."

"She tell you what she's up to?"

I wiped off the bubbles.

"No. I've left her three messages. Nothing."

This was a real sore point with me. Bertie had gotten herself together. But some things had stayed the same. I was still one name on her list of folks to tap when she wanted something. It wasn't, "Hi, Mom, how are you?" it was, "Mom, what can you do for me today?" I hadn't heard from her since she'd mentioned that she thought it would be a good idea for me to keep T for a few months, just how many months she didn't say. Then she said that she needed to know my decision by the fifteenth. The fifteenth or what? Not real encouraging.

Jess was quiet.

"There's Rashawn . . ."

"Juanita, there's nothing you can do for that boy. He's gonna have to take care of this himself."

"I know, I know," I said, feeling my voice getting smaller and smaller. "But I'm still his mother. I just wish . . ." I had been wishing on that same star since Rashawn was thirteen and it just blinked back at me silently. Maybe it was the wrong star.

Jess moved the warm water across me in waves with his hand. It was soothing.

"It's hard to watch the mistakes from the sidelines," he said, quietly.

"No kidding."

"And there's one more thing," Jess offered.

I had taken up a handful of bubbles and was blowing on them to see if they would float across the room like the bubbles did when we were kids.

"No, that's all," I said. *That's enough.*

"When were you going to tell me that you're goin' back to school?"

"Did you open the . . ." He was grinning at me. No, he hadn't opened the white envelope. He'd just tricked me into telling him what it was all about.

"I haven't decided yet," I lied.

"Yeah, right. Well, you'd better hurry up. The term begins pretty soon, doesn't it?"

I knew that. I'd known that for weeks, months really. I knew exactly when the term started and the time of my first class and the name of the teacher: Banes. I also knew how long before I'd lose my deposit money if I dropped out. That's assuming that I'd gotten *in.* When I told Jess that, he almost turned on the cold water.

"Why the hell would you drop out?"

"Because . . . I can't . . . go," I heard Millie's voice in my ear. *"Of course, you can!"*

"Why the hell not?" Jess bellowed.

I sat up in the tub. Despite the glow of the candles, the mood had been broken.

Jess shrugged his shoulders as he reached for a towel.

"There ain't no way. I've got the diner . . ."

"Juanita, you are indispensable but we have your recipes, the diner gets along just fine without you. All you have to do is," he tickled me, "make a celebrity appearance once in a while."

"OK, then there's the inn. I have to manage the place. And with school, too . . ." I frowned. I was afraid of having too many good choices after a hundred years of nothing but bad ones. What was wrong with me? My mind was spinning. Then, there was Teishia. I had told Bertie that I wasn't coming back to Columbus. But that wouldn't stop her from coming out here and leaving a three-year-old deposit on my doorstep. And then, there was Nina . . .

"It's too much for me. I can only do one thing at a time."

"Might be true if you're trying to be a one-woman armored tank and tough your way through. But if you ask for a little help, delegate (that's a new word), and not try to do every damn thing yourself, you might be surprised at what you can accomplish."

"But it's too hard! I'm too . . . stupid to do the course work. I barely got through high school, there's no way I'll survive all those classes at once!"

Jess's frown deepened until it completely turned his face almost inside out.

"Juanita, what classes are you taking exactly? Aerospace engineering?"

"Might as well be," I grumbled as I let the water out. "I've applied for the Culinary Arts program. Maybe . . . learn to be a pastry chef."

Jess sat back on his heels and stared at me, had a funny, unreadable look on his face.

"What? You don't think I can do it?" I asked him, starting to get angry. I didn't think I could do it either but I sure as hell didn't want him to agree with me.

"No . . . no, it ain't that," he said slowly. "It's just . . . well, I didn't know you were thinking about being a pastry chef."

I didn't know that I was thinking about it either until I went to Los Angeles. And then I couldn't think of anything else. I started remembering how Jess folded this, garnished that and, sometimes, made his own sausage. I thought about my son stir-frying a Cantonese–Italian "fusion" dish, as he called it. And watching him plate a meal so that it looked like a painting ready to be hung. I was fascinated by the way that Wendy sketched out, planned, and built her tasty creations: Measuring this and shaving off that and putting pieces together like Legos and Tinker Toys; swirling whipped cream made from scratch here and dropping a dollop of something else gooey and full of sugar and calories there; and creating the right balance of structure and lightness in pastry crusts. It was amazing. It looked like fun. It looked like art. To me, it had the same appeal that playing in the mud has for a little kid. But I am just a homegrown kind of cook, not a chef, not a gourmet, not a certified anything. But I wanted to be certified and qualified. A woman with . . . credentials.

"It sounds good until you add in everything else," I told Jess.

He listened for a moment but I could tell that his mind was working.

"A chef . . . how long is the program? A year?"

When I told him, he whistled.

"That's a serious time commitment," he said thoughtfully. He handed me a pair of elephant-sized towels. "Dry off. I'll be right back."

"Well, what do you think?" I yelled after he'd been gone a few moments.

"Sounds like the diner is going to have soufflés, flambés, petits fours, and tarts on the menu to go along with the rest of my cuisine," he answered, and then appeared in the doorway. "Or, are you planning to ply your trade in a celebrity haven like New York City or Las Vegas? Or maybe a fancy cruise ship?"

"I don't know what I'm going to do with it," I admitted. I hadn't thought that far ahead, it was just too exhausting to think about these days. I sighed as I slipped on my robe. "I gotta get through the classes first."

"Aw, you can do it," he told me. "You been accepted yet?"

I paused.

"I don't know. I'm afraid to open the envelope and find out."

Jess gave me a look that said "You got to be kidding me!" but he didn't say anything. Just sat me down on the bed, put my feet up on a stool, and pulled two bottles of nail polish out of his pocket.

"Passionate Pearlized Plum or Feathered Fanny's Fuchsia?"

"What? What are you doing?"

He grinned as he waved a nail file in the air like a conductor leading an orchestra.

"I already *told* you. I'm going to give you a pedicure."

Now it was my turn to give him the you've-got-to-be-kidding-me look.

"Where did you learn to do a pedicure?"

Jess threw his hair over his shoulder (with a flourish) and began to file the nail on my big toe.

"I'm not a Philistine. In fact, the Philistines weren't bad folks at all. I saw it on the History Channel. And, for your information, I learned all about giving spa pedicures on the Lifestyle and Leisure Channel. Picked up all the tips, from polish changes to sanding down corns."

He slipped on his reading glasses and turned my left foot around in his hands as if he was studying a laboratory mouse. I tried, without any luck at all, to take my foot away from him.

"We can talk about my corns another time . . . Jess! Stop!"

Now, he was kissing my foot—one toe at a time. I closed my eyes.

"Feathered Fuchsia's Fanny . . ." I murmured. "I thought you were going to give me a pedicure." His hands weren't anywhere near my feet now. And I had completely forgotten about cooking classes, Sedona, will bequests, temperamental ghosts, or the corns on my little toe.

"We can talk about that another time," he said.

Best pedicure I ever had. And I didn't even get my toenails painted.

Later, much later, in the dark, when I was drifting off to sleep, I thought I heard Jess say, "Open the envelope, Juanita."

Chapter Eight

"Dear Ms. Louis,

We are pleased to inform you of your acceptance to the Culinary Arts Chef Program of Arcadia Valley Community and Technical College . . ."

I read the acceptance letter to Jess with a sinking feeling in my stomach.

"Oh, no, I can't go to school."

"What's your problem, Juanita? This is a good thing," Jess said, his forehead wrinkled in confusion at my reaction.

"Oh, no, it isn't," I said, as much to myself as to him. "What do I do now?"

Jess gave me a you-need-to-get-over-this look and continued to look over the letter.

"According to this, you send them the money for the deposit, get your supplies, and take your carcass over there on the tenth, ready to get to work. Sounds pretty simple to me."

My panic had moved to another level. I was reading the textbook list.

Textbooks! These were humongous, multipaged, heavy-looking volumes that cost a lot of money! And they weren't just cookbooks. These were *school*books. To be used for people who were . . . students.

"I just wanted to cook," I murmured. Jess wasn't paying much attention to me.

"Hmm . . . looks like we'll have to make a run to the restaurant supply store in Missoula to get you the proper chef's gear. Impressive." He nodded his head in approval. "Arcadia Valley. I had forgotten that they'd started a culinary arts program."

"I don't know why you're so happy about this," I snapped at him. I felt like an idiot for opening up this can of worms. Who did I think I was? Going back to school. Fear made me start talking like a fool.

"I'm not going," I told Jess. "Did you see that course list? Mathematics? Business principles? Restaurant management, part one? I thought that we were just going to cook, bake a few things. Roll out pie dough, throw together éclairs or something . . ." I felt like a second grader skipping third grade to go to high school.

Jess tried to keep his expression serious but he wasn't any good at it. He folded up the letter and put it back in the envelope. He looked at me as if I was stupid. Maybe I was.

"You don't *throw* an éclair together, Juanita. I hate to have to tell you this, but I think you know it already. This chef thing you're about to get into? It ain't like whipping up a sweet potato pie or making a pot of beef stew. You will learn techniques and the science behind the simmer. This is heavy-duty, serious-ass cuisine."

Cuisine? I don't want to do cuisine!

"I just wanted to . . . bake something." I sighed. It was going to be worse than I thought.

"I kind of envy you," Jess said. Now, he wasn't paying any attention to me at all. "I remember taking this stuff in New York back before Jesus wore long robes." He smiled so I guess his memories were good ones. All I could see ahead of me was a nightmare. "In my first baking class, we made croissants . . . mine were . . . tough. Too much yeast. Or was it too little?" He frowned as he tried to remember. I was beyond caring about this pleasant little romp down memory lane. "Measurements, design, precision . . . yeah, that's the word, precision. There's no pinch of this and handful of that. Pastry is all about precision." He tapped the table with the palm of his hand to make his point.

Precision. Wonderful.

"I thought I was learning to be a chef, not an engineer." Jess couldn't help himself now, he just grinned.

"Being a chef *is* being an engineer. You are an engineer of food."

Oh, great. This is what I get for being a wild woman adventuress, I said to myself. *Believing all that crap I've been reading. Just jumping into things, feet first, without looking. I get . . . precision.*

No one was sympathetic.

"That's perfect, darling!" Nina gushed over the phone. "And my cousin says she'll sign the papers as soon as she returns from the Galápagos!"

Things only got worse when I visited the school. I met with the program director. His name was Heinrich. He smiled and led me into an office that was just off the white and stainless-steel kitchen classroom that was so big it made our voices echo.

"I like to meet with all the prospective students," Heinrich said, looking at a piece of paper. *Oh, oh, I thought, he's probably reading my file and wondering how the hell I ever got into his program.* "Is important to find out their motivations, likes, and dislikes."

My throat closed up.

I think I told him, "I just want to cook." And, bless his heart, I think old Heinrich understood that. In fact, our entire conversation went pretty well, I think, until . . .

"You are an instinctive cook, Madame Louis," he said, his brown eyes serious. "A good cook, I hear, but instinctive. You will have to set that aside for a while during this course. You will have to take that head away." *Head?* "All of your old formulas, they go into the dustbin."

"My . . . formulas?" Was this the chemistry department?

The program director gave me a boy-have-you-got-a-lot-to-learn smile.

"Ya. Your formulas. What you call 'recipes,' in this class, they are formulas."

I *had* walked into the chemistry department.

I felt even worse when I observed the classes.

In the first place, I am, on the outside, at *least* one hundred years older than most of the students, including one kid who, I'm sure, wasn't even shaving yet. In the second place, I am at least fifty years older than the instructor. That's not good either. Last, but absolutely not least, these folks were cooking and baking dishes that I had barely even heard of, even *with* Jess's nouvelle Montana cuisine.

"All right, people," bellowed Chef Durphy. He loomed over the shoulder of one poor soul who was making a righteous mess of something that she was pouring into an oblong dish. He gave her a look that would melt lead, then proceeded with his lecture. "Every one of you would be fired for leaving the counters like this. Clean up after yourselves—that's an order! Quickly now!"

White coats flew this way and that.

"Hot pan!" one infant warned, carrying a small, steaming saucepan toward the dish room.

"Mind the knives," countered another.

With military precision, they moved this way and that as they chopped, sautéed, poured, and puréed. Mixers buzzed, saucepans sizzled, and terrines (whatever the hell they are) were gently set to rest in a whale-sized vat of hot water, then put into the ovens.

"Whose materials are these?" Chef barked out.

The chopping, pouring, whizzing, and sautéing continued. Only one set of eyes looked up. Guilty as hell. Chef's brow furrowed and his face darkened. I could tell that the mark in the grade book wouldn't be a good one. The guilty party scooped up the bowls, dirty spoons, and cutting board and scurried off to the dish room.

"I can't imagine any of you working in any place other than Betty's Hot Dog Stand! This is deplorable! What's happened here?" The terrine was dripping down the sides of the casserole dish. "Make sure it's clean before you put it into the oven."

The orders, interrogation, scurrying, and scampering continued. I sneaked a quick glance at the other prospective students who were also observing the class. They were enthralled. I was petrified. I thought I had enrolled in a culinary arts program, not the U.S. Army! The kitchen was scrubbed until it was spotless and everything, from the largest mixing bowl to the tiniest paring knife, was back in its place. I felt as if I had just observed a strategic military exercise. There wasn't any leisurely stirring of chili or calm, easy seasoning of a roast. This was like . . . well, it was like an army mission.

Juanita Louis, home-style cook and barely-made-it-through-high-school graduate.

Yep. I was in deep, deep trouble now.

"He calls recipes 'formulas!'" I wailed to Jess that evening. "The students move like lightning! Everything is so . . . precise! So . . . regimented. All these steps to everything: peeling, cutting, melting, sieving, adding, chopping, basting, measuring . . ."

"I think you have them out of order." Jess said. "After a week, you'll get the hang of it."

"I need a drink," I said, sinking deeper into the sofa cushions in his front room.

"Juanita, you don't drink," Jess said matter-of-factly. "You want some tea or something?"

"Yeah . . . tea. Throw rat poison in it, will you?" I mumbled.

"Quit being a drama queen," he yelled back as he moved down the hall. "I keep telling you, you can do this."

That's what Wendy said. That's what Millie would have said. What did they know?

Dracula landed with a thump beside me and put his heavy head in my lap. I was so distracted that I didn't pay attention to the slobber that he brought with him.

You say a prayer, wish upon a star, cross your fingers, and rub a rabbit's foot. And then, when your dream, your prayer comes true, you panic. Another one of God's games? I said I had wanted credentials. Now, I was going to get them. And more.

When the gods wish to punish us, they answer our prayers.

I have a better saying. When God wants to punish you, he sends you every darned thing at once.

"You need to get over that new-life nonsense, Momma," Bertie had said. "Your life is back here—in Columbus."

There were a lot of reasons that Bertie felt this would be "the best thing" for me. But the main reason was because she wanted me to take care of Teishia. She left me a phone message about this and then we played phone tag for a while. Well, *I* played phone tag. Bertie called me back after I'd left her five messages.

"Hey, Ma," she said in a crisp voice. "When are you coming? Lee and I can pick you up at the airport." Lee was her new boyfriend.

"Bertie, didn't you get my message?" Messages, I should have said.

"Yeah," was her one-word response.

OK. Was I crazy? Or was she?

"Bertie, I left you a message, several as a matter of fact. I have a lot of responsibilities, things going on *here*." Already, I was making excuses to her for having a life of my own. I felt my world tilting sideways with me hanging on by my fingernails.

"Oh," was the next one-word response. Like I'd just told her it was raining and to bring an umbrella. "Well, you need to be here before the twentieth of May, 'cause me and T . . ." She hadn't heard a word I'd said.

"The twentieth!" I squealed. "That's in six weeks! You think that I'm just gonna show up there on the twentieth? And stay for how long, Bertie?"

She sighed as loudly as a person can.

"I don't know, Momma. For a couple months anyway."

I don't usually get headaches but my head felt as if it was being pounded by a sledgehammer.

"Momma, I *told* you that I was gonna need you to take T for me." Bertie spoke slowly and sounded out every syllable as if she was talking to somebody stupid. "I *told* you that. *You know* I got a break coming up and I'm working two jobs. Now are you gonna take T for me, or not?"

Now, it was my turn to sigh.

Teishia is a normal, active little kid, full of laughter and chatter. She likes puppets and she likes to play in the dirt and crumple up newspaper because the sound makes her giggle. But, you see, Teishia ain't the problem.

Bertie is.

Now it's time for me to decide if Bertie is *my* problem—or not.

They call them "flashbacks." I have these waking nightmares once in a while but one really stays with me. I break out in a cold sweat because the sound of a little kid's voice or a baby crying will bring back the memory—sounds, smells, worry, everything.

Teishia was a year old, maybe a little more, maybe less. I was working at the hospital, three to eleven. Came home late one Friday night because I missed the last bus and had to call a cab. Bertie damn near knocked me down as I walked in the door. She was right in my face, dressed up, hair done, perfume, even had the purse in her hand. She was ready to go. It was twelve-thirty at night. She greeted me . . . no, "greet" is not the right word. She met me at the door with the attitude of somebody who has just been robbed of something—her valuable time.

"It's about time you got here! I was s'posed to be outa here an hour ago!"

This was the first time I'd heard that I was babysitting.

"Where you goin'?" I asked. I had to push by her to get inside the apartment.

Bertie sighed loudly and rolled her eyes. Her girl-friend, whose name I have forgotten—they've all blurred together—rolled her eyes, too. Both of the girls snickered.

"Out," she said bluntly, pushing by me. She brought her arm around with a wide sweep and pointedly looked at her watch. Correction, *my* watch that she'd borrowed from me a while ago and had not returned. "And I'm late. See you later."

It seems hard to believe now that I let her talk to me like that, treat me like that, but you can't undo what's past. You either rewind it or do something about it. Back then, I just took what she dished out and yelled after her, "T asleep?" At twelve-thirty, the answer should have been obvious, but with Bertie, you never knew. Sometimes, I came in from work at night and that baby was still in her play-clothes, wide awake.

"Yeah, she's in the playpen," Bertie yelled back from the second flight of stairs. Her voice echoed off the dirty lime green–colored walls. The girls chattered on their way down the stairs and I heard their laughter, then the heavy outside door to the building slammed and there was si-lence.

I closed the door, clicked off the TV, and looked at T. She was sleeping, which was amazing considering how loud the TV had been and how much noise Bertie and her friend had been making. My heart sank when I noticed that the baby was still wearing her day clothes complete with a bib that had food stains on it. I'd have to nominate my daughter for the Mother of the Year Award before someone else did.

Bertie didn't call until Sunday, when she called to let me know she was "on her way." I heard a party going on in the background. By 11:30 AM Monday, Bertie was still "on the way." My sister, KayRita, closes her beauty shop on Mondays so she babysat T so that I could go to work. Bertie left a message that she'd gotten "hung up" and would be "by later." She finally came home on Tuesday.

KayRita gave me an earful.

"Juanita, I don't know what's wrong with you. I woulda taken that gal's head off and mopped up the floor with it. Kicked her butt from here to Cleveland." I heard the sound of water in the background. I could see my sister balancing the phone between her shoulder and ear as she shampooed her customer. "You need to have a come-to-Jesus meeting with Bertie. I don't know why you put up with that mess."

But when Bertie came in that afternoon, I was so worn out and worried half to death that I was exhausted. It took all my energy to look at her and then walk out of that door and catch my bus. I was relieved that she was alive and not beaten up, raped, or left dead somewhere. I was angry about her just leaving the baby with no concern at all about how she was or how long she'd be gone or any damn thing. But I was tired. When you're weary, nothing else seems to matter much. The life and the spirit have just plain dripped out of you.

But I am not that woman anymore.

"Momma! You hear me?"

"I hear you," I told her. "Bertie, I've got to go. I'm real sorry about this, but I won't be able to take Teishia. You'll have to make other plans."

I heard her take in a breath and then she called me a really ugly name in a voice as cold as a glacier.

"I don't have to listen to that disrespect." I had my finger on the button.

"But she's *your* granddaughter!" Bertie exclaimed as if

that would make it all right for her to call me names and try to run a guilt trip on my head.

"She is *your* daughter," I said.

"Have you lost your mind?" she yelled.

"Oh, no. But you must have lost yours, thinking you're just going to drop that child on me with hardly any notice or anything. I have to go. I'll talk with you another time . . ." *No time soon.*

"I don't give a shit what you have planned, I *could* just fly out there and leave Teishia."

Poor Teishia, that she should have such a mother.

There's a sci-fi movie that I saw once, peeking through my fingers because it was so scary. It's about a space monster that starts out as a parasite. It grows inside you and then pops out and makes a nasty mess. This thing is the ugliest damn monster you ever saw with a face stretched back tight over its skull and a mouth full of big, sharp, drippy teeth. I think it eats its young, too. Not a bad idea. This monster came out of me when I was talking with Bertie. I know this because Dracula whined and took off out of the room with his tail between his legs.

"Bertie, you do that, you'd better run fast 'cause I'll be after you. I'll track you down if I have to walk across this country barefoot."

I hung up.

Guilt can be aggravating; it doesn't let you off the hook, no matter which way you go. If I took Teishia, everyone would be happy. Everyone but me. Of course, as far as Bertie is concerned, my happiness doesn't count. And, if I take Teishia, will Bertie ever learn to be responsible for her own daughter—good times or bad? And, if I don't take Teishia, folks will say that I'm being selfish and throwing off my responsibilities. I know that I'm family and I'm the grandmother. And I agree, it *does* take a village to bring up a child. But I have noticed that, even in villages, the older women *teach* the younger ones how to be mothers. I am the teacher but I don't know what lesson plan to use: the one that lightens the load for the burro or the one that helps the burro get strong enough to carry it. Way too many questions. No good answers.

After the first day of school, I was able to take one question off my list. I was not ready for school.

Chef Durphy had us sit in a semicircle around the sparkling stainless-steel tables. I looked like a chocolate Pillsbury doughwoman, dressed in white from head to toe. There were eighteen of us and we were supposed to introduce ourselves. By the time they got around to me, I felt as if I was six inches tall. A few of the students had a college degree. One of them had two! Many of 'em had worked in restaurants for years and were already chefs, not like me. I'm just a home-style cook. There were others who worked for corporations. And, to make it all worse, except for the instructor, I was the oldest thing in the room, and that included the desks and chairs!

"Karen Chin. I'm from San Francisco. B.A. from Pepperdine, Masters in Sociology from UC, Berkeley. I work for Kraft, in the product development division . . ."

"Larry Barrymore. I've been the sous-chef at Phenom for a year . . ."

"Brad Weeks. Hey, I went to Pepperdine, too, 1993. Did you know Linn Frazier?"

"Marti Dinsmore . . . U of M . . . Masters in Chemistry from . . . I'm taking the program as part of a company initiative . . ."

"Hello, I'm Juanita Louis, general diploma from Columbus East Central High School, twenty years of regular cooking, most recently the breakfast cook at the Paper Moon Diner, Paper Moon, Montana, and the Silver Cactus Hacienda in Sedona, Arizona."

Yeah, that's what I said. It's all that I could think of. Chef just smiled and said, "Next?" The person beside me began to speak.

Maybe they wouldn't notice me shrinking down to six inches tall and I could make a break for the door. Finally, the last infant was speaking so my torture was almost over. Then the voice of a young man broke the cycle.

"Hey, Juanita . . . Juanita Louis? You cook at the Paper Moon Diner, right?"

"Right," I said slowly. *Why, did I give you food poisoning?*

"Yeah, I thought I recognized you," the kid continued. He looked as if he was about ten years old with Howdy Doody red hair and freckles. Skinny as a sapling. "I go there sometimes with my cousins, the Manns? They live out just past Mason. I had some of your fried peach pies." He grinned and his freckles spread. "Man, they were awesome."

"Oh, yeah! I went there once, had something with shitake mushrooms on top . . ."

No, that wasn't mine.

"Did you make the chili? Best I've ever had except for my mom's . . ."

By some strange coincidence, I'd fixed lunch or breakfast for most of the other folks in the room. They were all nodding at me with smiles. The redheaded kid was grinning. Like growing boys everywhere, he is always hungry and never gains an ounce. "That meatloaf was sweet."

The instructor interrupted but smiled at me.

"Well, Madame Louis," he said with his clipped accent. "Your reputation has preceded you. Now we shall see if you can apply those skills to terrines and puffed pastry."

Oh, oh. What is a puffed out pastry?

Chapter Nine

When the gods want to punish us, they send every darned thing at once.

The day after I stayed up nearly all night to study for my first Food Sanitation and Safety test, Broderick Tilson Hayward-Smith showed up on the doorstep of Millie's place—four weeks early. Geoff Black managed to get me some advance notice—a few hours. Nice of him. Not only had I had a test that morning, but I'd also had a cooking project in Basic Baking class—our team assignment was honey-wheat bread. There were two of us: the redheaded kid, Marc, and me. The loaves looked like works of art when they came out of the oven: lightly golden brown on top, softly browned on the sides. They smelled like angels had baked them. Even Chef was forced to admit they looked and smelled perfect. We were so proud, until Marc tried to cut a slice. The loaf was doughy in the middle, wet, drippy, and gooey-looking. The baking angels had either forgotten to convert the formula correctly or they'd set the oven temperature wrong. Either way, our team got an "E" for effort and an "F" for the rest.

But even that was better than "the great salami disaster" of Basic Cooking One class the day before. Each team was assigned a salami or sausage to make—from seasoning, grinding, chopping, and mixing to squeezing, er, pushing, um, forcing the meat through the sausage grinder into the casings. Chef demonstrated a few times with Karen Chin's perfectly seasoned-blended-mixed andouille sausage then turned the grinder over to the students. Karen volunteered to go first. Of course. And her links came out ready to be photographed for a magazine layout. Chef oohed and aahed over them. The rest of us wanted to put Karen, instead of the sausage, through the grinder. When it was my turn, Marc and I flipped a coin to see who was going to do the grinding and who was going to handle the sausage casings. We both lost.

I don't know if you've ever seen one but an old-time commercial-grade iron sausage grinder looks like something left over from the Inquisition. I'd just finished reading a romance set during that period—those folks had no sense of humor at all. The grinder's big, it has a huge, cranklike handle, and it looks scary. It's as if some efficiency expert found a stash of these damn things in somebody's basement and said, "Don't throw them out! Use them to make sausage!"

So one of you cranks and one of you fills the casings. You have to make sure that you keep the casings good and snug around the meat mixture. If you're cranking, you have to make sure that you don't crank too slowly. And you have to make sure that you don't crank too fast.

"Faster," Marc said. His brow was scrunched up and his

eyes were fixed on the tube where the meat was coming into the sausage casing. He looked like a ballplayer waiting on the next pitch. I cranked faster.

"No, slower," he barked.

I cranked slower. The handle turned sluggishly as if I was crunching through somebody's bones and the tibia got stuck. Like I said, this thing was left over from the Inquisition.

"Faster, no . . ."

Well, all I heard was "faster," so faster it was.

The salami mixture broke through the casing and flew across the room, landing with a "splat" on the front of Julia's chef coat. The class broke up. Marc grinned for the rest of the day. Chef said, "Madame Louis, I suppose I shall have to order bulletproof vests for this class." He was only half kidding.

And now I had to deal with Hayward Tilson Smith or whatever his name was.

My mother said not to be "ugly" about things. Nina tells her clients that negative energy is a waste. But just once, I'd like to stir up a cauldron of eyes of snake or ear of toad (something like that) and mess up somebody good. Let's face it, some people do deserve it. I'm not like that. But *if* I were? I would have had to tell Millie "I'm sorry" 'cause I would have hacked Broderick Tilson Hayward-Smith into pieces and buried him under the rose bushes along the white picket fence. He was the biggest hemorrhoid that you ever met. And that is no lie.

He was a rude, arrogant, finicky, pompous ass. And those were the good things that I could say about him. He blew into Paper Moon, Montana like a plague of locusts and, within one week, he'd made himself as welcome as the stink coming off a landfill in the middle of August. Everybody, their brother, and their dog, wanted that man to leave town by sundown. I'd heard from the manager of the Bi-Lo, who'd heard from one of the nurses at the hospital, who was dating one of Millie's nephews, that Hayward-Smith had turned up his pointed nose at the invitations from his Tilson relatives. Even Elva Van Roan's patience wore thin. She locked the bathroom door on him one night and switched the lamps on and off in another room and I didn't have the heart to yell at her for it.

First old white man I ever saw with an entourage as large as a hip-hop star's. I heard through the grapevine that he'd flown into Missoula in a private jet. My, my. Rolled up to Millie's in a motorcade of three black Suburbans with tinted windows. He marched up the steps like a general (pretty spry for an old fart), followed by Williams, his valet, a skinny, pale-skinned man who looked like the cousin of Dracula, and Ms. Amy Hsu, his executive assistant, a four-foot-tall Tasmanian devil who wore glasses as big as an owl's eyes and black high-heeled boots.

Hayward-Smith walked through the front door without a knock, a push of the doorbell, or a "Hello, how are you? Kiss my big white butt." Just like he owned the place already. He looked at Inez and me over his nose as if we were ants and needed a squirt of Raid. Miz Hsu and Williams tried to look important, too, but they weren't as good at it as the old man was.

"I'm Broderick Hayward-Smith," he announced in a loud voice with an accent that sounded half English and half something else.

Well, no shit, I said to myself. *I thought I'd been waiting for the Easter Bunny.*

"You may address me as Mr. Hayward-Smith."

Oh, no, he didn't say that.

"I'm Juanita Louis," I told him in my best eastside Columbus, Ahia tones. "And *you* can call me Mrs. Louis." I almost said, "And you can kiss my wide brown behind," but I left that part out.

I don't think Mr. H-Smith (one of the more flattering names that I would call him behind his back from that day on) was ready for me. And I wasn't ready for him either. I was expecting someone who was funny and friendly like Millie. I had forgotten that, even though he was Millie's son, she hadn't raised him. And he must have been expecting a Laura Ashley dress, clogs, and blonde hair. So we were both disappointed.

Broderick Tilson Hayward-Smith is as tall and as wide as Mountain and, like Mountain, he has blue eyes—his mother's blue eyes. He probably had blonde hair when he was young, like most of the other Tilsons around here. But that's where the similarities end. Mountain has a wide open face, like the eastern plains of Montana; there is friendliness, gullibility, and a whole lot of humor there. Broderick's nostrils pinch together and the tip of his nose curls up as if he just came across a pile of something Dracula left in the middle of the floor. The corners of his mouth curve down. Makes him look like Abel's bloodhound, Trixie. The man hasn't smiled in forty years. He has the expression of someone who needs a good . . . let's just say I think he needs a laxative. A *strong* laxative.

His eyebrows rose slightly when I introduced myself. He didn't expect *me* to be the Juanita Louis who was mentioned in his mother's will. I smiled and pointed his roadies (or whoever they were) toward the banister. They were loaded up with suitcases, office equipment, and boxes. It was bad enough that he'd come early—how long was he planning to stay?

"Up the stairs, down the hall, take the back staircase," I told them sweetly. "That will take you to the third floor."

To Mr. Pointy Nose Tight Ass, I said, "We've given you the Tower Suite, *Mister* Hayward-Smith. It's our largest and most luxurious accommodation. You'll be *very* comfortable there." I smiled as widely as I knew how.

Inez cleared her throat but I ignored her. Until just ten seconds ago, Mister H-Smith was going to the Monte Carlo Room, a spacious room on the second floor that catches the morning sun. Next to the Mauve Room, it is my favorite, with its French country decor and wood-burning fireplace.

But the man had ticked me off with his ski-slope nose and stuck-up behind. He may be able to prove that Millie was a little crazy—I don't know if Geoff Black will be able to prove that she wasn't. But until that hearing, I'm the inn-keeper, and Mr. High-Up Butt goes in the Tower Suite with the ghost.

"Thank you, Mrs. Louis. I'm sure that it will be adequate."

I watched him climb the stairs.

Inez was giggling.

I hoped that Elva Van Roan didn't take me seriously when I asked her to behave. I was only kidding.

I know cooking. I can clean pretty well if I have to, and I make a dynamite nurse's aide. But what I don't know about running a business would fit in the Superdome. But I am a fast learner. Thank God for Millie. Despite her frilly and impractical appearance, the woman had a head for business. She had organized it all in a notebook, scheduling each activity of the bed and breakfast, from rotating towels and sheets to sending out thank-you notes. Her accounts were set up on the computer, and she had mailing lists prepared and contact lists for anything that might go wrong with the house, from plumbing to ghost therapy. All I had to do was follow her instructions and keep it simple. I was also learning how to use a computer, but I keep pressing "delete" instead of "enter."

"This is a bed-and-breakfast," Millie had said months before when I suggested that she serve sandwiches or dinner. "We can't be all things to all people. You've got to make a choice about what you want to do and then do the very best you can at it." Looking back on that conversation, I realize now that she wasn't just talking about running a business.

Inez, Gwen, and I kept the linens changed, the bathrooms clean, and the breakfasts cooked. We answered the phone, Inez handled e-mail, and I . . . well, I managed. I am happy to say that it worked. At least it did most of the time. There was just one hitch. We didn't count on having the houseguest from hell.

"He is like the man who comes to dinner," Inez said under her breath. "We'll be stuck with him forever." That was one old movie of Millie's that I hadn't seen. But I did remember what old Ben Franklin said. Something about fish, houseguests, and three days. Most of the B&B guests stayed only about two or three nights. Hayward-Smith and group would be with us for more than four weeks. If they'd been fish filets the place would stink to high heaven.

Smith and company took over the inn. They set up computers, a fax machine, and a copier. Williams, the valet, commandeered the back pantry and turned it into an "ironing room" since Mr. H-Smith liked his stiff, white-on-white button-down shirts "just so" and the local dry cleaners couldn't be relied on to do that. I can't imagine why—they did OK when they put creases into blue jeans. Williams looks like the creepy butler in old black-and-white horror movies, the ones that are on at two in the morning. Tall and thin, with dark, slicked-back hair, Williams is the color of rice pudding that's been cooked too long—not white, not quite beige, not pink but very waxy looking. And serious. If he smiled, his face would split and crack. I imagined him turning into a vampire bat and flying around a turret.

"I am responsible for Mr. Hayward-Smith's person," he told me.

All righty.

Miz Hsu, a little bit of a person who moved like a hummingbird and always had one of those palm thingies in her hand, took care of everything business related, whatever business Mr. Pointy Nose was into. If she wasn't tapping on her notebook-sized computer, she had a cell phone to her ear, sometimes two of them. Amy is attractive and very stylish with her huge hoop earrings and short, deep burgundy-colored spiked hair. She doesn't wear anything but black. Inez, who knows about these things, says that her suits are very expensive. She's crazy about three-inch-heeled boots. Watching her skip up and down the stairs was enough to cause you heart palpitations. Inez and I took bets on which one of us would have to drive her over to County Medical when she tripped and broke something.

Both of these characters acted like their poop didn't

stink, but at least they were pretty easy to please. Williams was happy with one industrial-sized cup of black coffee in the morning to give him a jump-start, and he had no complaints about the Violet Room. And Ms. Hsu was a girl who would have been right at home at Nina's hacienda in Sedona. You could cook her up a Belgian waffle with fresh strawberries on it and crisp bacon on the side and that gal would take two bites of everything and say she was full. No wonder she was the size of a half minute.

Mr. High-Up Butt was something else.

He didn't even start *out* on the good foot. Just pissed me off right away and it went downhill from there. First off, he was the pickiest man I ever met. I'm not talking about wanting to have things a certain way; I'm used to that from taking care of patients. Running a bed-and-breakfast is the same way. People like to be around the things that make them comfortable. But Hayward-Smith? Let's just say that I'm surprised that he's managed to make his first million considering the amount of time he spends worrying about the way that the window shades are drawn.

I know that "God is in the details." But I maintain that He never would have had time to create the earth if he had still been worrying about how many grains of sand he'd put on the beach and whether they were perfectly shaped and aligned.

The first evening that Mr. High-Up Butt stayed at Millie's, he sent Williams down with all the towels from the bathroom.

"Mr. Williams?" I said. I had to make sure it was him since his face was completely hidden by a tower of stacked towels.

"Mr. Hayward-Smith only uses white towels, ma'am.

And he prefers that they be folded in half first, then, like so, on the sides." Williams demonstrated.

"I see," I told him. I said this with a smile.

Fifteen minutes later, he was back.

"May I help you, Mr. Williams?" Yes, I was still smiling.

"Uh, just 'Williams,' Mrs. Louis. Mr. Hayward-Smith wanted to remind you that he only drinks bottled water. Evian. If he could have a few bottles for the bathroom, ma'am, to brush his teeth."

"Of course," I said. Now would he really know the difference between Evian and Meagher County Reservoir? My smile was starting to hurt my cheeks.

Williams returned ten minutes later. I was trying to make heads or tails of my homework. I wasn't having much luck. This time, Williams coughed to get my attention.

"Yes, Mr., er, Williams?" My smile was fading fast.

"Mr. Hayward-Smith wanted me to confirm that the pillows are hypoallergenic."

"Yessss," I told him. Now, I was counting to twenty. Mr. High-Up Butt had faxed over a page of his "requirements" prior to his early and unexpected arrival. The pillow requirement was on the list. The Evian water was not.

By the time I left for the night, Williams had run down and up three flights of stairs—four more times. "Mr. Hayward-Smith will have Earl Grey tea and unbuttered rye toast for breakfast. Served at seven-thirty sharp."

"Mr. Hayward-Smith requires that his hand towels be changed twice daily."

"Mr. Hayward-Smith wants his FedEx packages brought to him immediately."

"Does Mr. Hayward-Smith want single-ply or double-ply toilet paper?" I asked. "You don't know? Oh, then

maybe I'd better ask him myself. I wouldn't want him to ir-
ritate his backside." I headed for the stairs.

Williams followed me, protesting.

"Ma'am, I really don't think . . . what I mean is, Mr.
Hayward-Smith doesn't . . . he's not quite decent, ma'am."

But I took the steps almost two at a time. I had had Mr.
H-Smith over my head and he hadn't been in the house
more than twenty-four hours. I was through with the
back-and-forth stuff. If Mr. High-Up Butt wanted something done, then he needed to talk with me. Directly. I
knocked on his door.

"Come in."

I opened the door. H-Smith was at the desk in the sitting room, peering at a computer screen.

"Mr. Hayward-Smith," I said, pronouncing every syllable as slowly as I could just as he did. "Mr. Williams, here,
has a list of items that you . . . require. Maybe you'd like to
go over your list now? So that I can take care of everything all at once. Would that be OK with you?"

"Oh, it's you. Um, Louis . . ." He always looked at me
as if I was a fly he'd just smashed on the end of the fly-
swatter.

"*Mrs.* Louis," I said. *Thank-you, Rodney Louis, wherever you
are.*

"Yes. Right. I think Williams has taken care of everything that I require. Thank-you, um, Mrs. Louis." I turned
to leave when Hayward-Smith's voice came again. "Oh,
there was one more item."

I started counting to twenty-five right then.

"I would like to review the luncheon and dinner menus,
Mrs. Louis. They weren't on the desk with the breakfast
menu."

"That's because we are a bed-and-breakfast, Mr. Hayward-Smith," I told him. *"Your mother* ran the inn that way." He winced when I said "your mother" and I wondered why. "We only serve breakfast. I did include a listing of local restaurants for your convenience. Most of them are pretty close by, just a few minutes drive, unless you want to go into Mason or Missoula. . . . Are you all right, Mr. Hayward-Smith?"

Both Williams and Mr. Pointy Nose High-Up Butt looked as if they were about to have strokes.

"Obviously, my *mother* had no business sense at all," Hayward-Smith said in a sharp tone.

I took that comment personally.

"I think she did just fine. In fact, I . . ." I started to say something else but remembered that Geoff Black had warned me not to be . . . what was the word he used? "Acrimonious." I had looked it up. It meant "caustic" or "biting." Yeah, I was about to tell Hayward-Smith what he could bite, all right.

"Oh, Mr. Hayward-Smith couldn't possibly go out to any . . . of those places," Williams gasped before his employer, or I, could say anything else. "Perhaps . . . they deliver?"

In my daydream, I could imagine Fred at Fred's Coney Island picking up the phone and being asked if he delivered. Or Jess, for that matter. The diner does a lot of things but it doesn't do delivery.

I shook my head and kept a straight face. Sort of.

"None of them deliver. And Missoula is a little far. But they do have carry-out."

Williams looked as if he was going to have a fainting attack but the suggestion must have appealed to him and to his employer because they agreed that would be acceptable. And I left that room before I got mad enough to start throwing sharp objects. For the next week, I hardly saw Mr. H-Smith at all and that was just fine with me. And I only spoke to Williams once more. This time, he had a request that had nothing to do with food.

"Mr. Hayward-Smith would like to have a tour of the house, if your schedule would permit, Mrs. Louis."

Great.

"So, you're going to give him the grand tour," Jess commented. He was prepping for dinner, chopping onions, peppers, and celery for a gumbo recipe that I had shared with him. He scraped the vegetables aside and started measuring the spices. His expression was mischievous. "I'd like to be a fly on the wall for that little event. Are you going to show him Millie's boudoir or is that still off limits?"

I was sitting on the stool in the kitchen watching him work and reading off the measurements. I've only made this dish a few thousand times but it can be tricky. Sometimes I have to throw the roux out because it is either too light or I've burned it.

"No, I'll show him her rooms. The attorney says it's OK to do that. I guess I'm just disappointed. . . . No, Jess. No filé, use the okra." Bobby Smith's experience with filé powder came back to me. It must have come back to Jess, too, because he chuckled. "I know what you're thinking. But the okra will help with the thickness."

As I supervised (Jess called it "meddling"), I thought about what Millie would have thought about Broderick Tilson Hayward-Smith, his stiff personality, and stuck-up way of talking. I couldn't imagine them getting along together. I wondered if they'd ever met when he was growing up. And I wondered why he seemed to hate her so much.

Mignon peeked around the kitchen door.

"Mountain's here," she said. "Can he still get some breakfast?"

"Yeah, what does he want, the usual?" I asked her. To Jess, I said, "I'll get it."

Mignon glanced at Jess and her smile dimmed slightly.

"Um, he'll have," she looked down at her pad, "one egg over easy, white toast, and coffee."

I watched her disappear. Mountain's usual breakfast order is three eggs, scrambled, grits (or hash browns, or both), six strips of bacon, two slices of toast (or three pancakes or one extra-large Belgian waffle), coffee, a large O.J., and beefsteak tomatoes, if they are in season.

If Mountain only ordered one egg and one slice of toast, that boy was either (a) dying or (b) already dead.

I left Jess in the kitchen chopping celery to find out which one it was.

"Don't be too hard on him," Jess called after me. "He's lovesick."

"You know anything about this?"

Jess shrugged his shoulders but kept his head down as he concentrated on his chopping.

"Yeah. I forgot to mention it."

Wonderful.

I found Mountain sitting at a table (not like him), alone (not at *all* like him), staring out of the window (*really* out of character). His arms were at his sides, his hands in his lap, and his elbows weren't on the table. I concluded right then and there that he was seriously ill.

Mountain looked real pitiful but I decided to tackle him head-on. When he looked up at me, I could see that he had lost weight. He actually had cheekbones.

"Mountain, since when do you eat one egg and a slice of white toast in my diner? You're going to hurt my feelings!"

"Oh, hey, Juanita," Mountain said without a smile or any feeling at all. He hardly looked at me. "Don't take it personally. I'm just not real hungry," he added.

"You need to eat enough to keep up your strength if you and that Swenson girl plan to keep dancing like you did at Millie's party."

I noticed Mignon just behind Mountain holding the coffeepot. She was shaking her head and mouthing the word, "No."

"Oh," Mountain's voice was low. "You've been so busy with school and Millie's place that you probably didn't know. Lawra dumped me."

Mignon rolled her eyes and poured his coffee. I wanted to drop through the floor.

"Oh, I'm real sorry to hear about that," I told him. "Let me fix up a nice Southwestern omelet for you or some French toast. You can't live on one scrambled egg." My solution to most traumas of the heart is to feed the stomach. It doesn't always work but at least it keeps you from feeling sorry for yourself *and* starving at the same time.

Mountain's eyes were sad like a kid who's been told that there isn't a Santa Claus.

"Thanks, but I'm not that hungry. Honest."

And he only ate that egg and half a piece of toast. Not what I expected from Mountain. One more thing to worry about. Peaches had come through the week before, her face a little gray, her eyes bleary. She'd barely eaten a full meal either.

"Peaches, you got the flu again?" I'd asked her.

Her smile barely lifted her cheeks.

"No . . . just a little tired. Long haul," she said in a voice that was low and slow and very much un-Peaches-like. The fact that she was having more tests done in Casper didn't make me feel any better. And she wasn't telling me or anyone what kind of tests they were.

And now, Mountain? I went back into the kitchen to find out what was going on.

"How long has he . . ."

"Shhhh!"

"I just wanted to know when Mountain . . ."

"Quiet!"

I stopped in the middle of the kitchen floor. Mignon had stopped, too, even though she had a tray of orders balanced on her hand.

"The chef is at work," she said sarcastically. "He needs . . . complete silence."

The "Chef" was a comical sight.

He had the Bull's cap on backward, his hair was hanging in a braid down his back, and he wore one pair of glasses while the other pair rested on top of the baseball cap. He was stirring something in the large cast-iron skillet. What-ever it was, it smelled wonderful. I looked over his shoul-der and smiled.

"Back off," he barked, shrugging me away. "This is the critical point in the roux. It is about to make the color change. I need my concentration."

"Jess, it's just flour and oil. You act as if you're doing a chemistry experiment."

He snorted. Not in the roux, thankfully.

"That's what's wrong with you, Juanita. No respect for the food. Everything has to be . . . just right. Precision, that's the word. Precision. Now watch this. And be quiet, will you?"

Good grief.

He stirred with machinelike precision and very slowly, almost like the change of day to night, the mixture began to thicken and changed color from a light caramel to a deep reddish brown. It was a pretty sight. When the roux was just the way he wanted it, he added the chopped vegetables and let them cook and soften.

"Now, I can be sociable," he said with relief, wiping his hands on his "Grouch in the Kitchen" apron that I had given him for Christmas.

"Since when have you ever been sociable? And when were you going to tell me about Mountain?"

Jess shrugged as he grabbed a can of Coke.

"Thought I'd get around to it sooner or later. It wasn't real high up on the crisis list this week. I figured you had enough to deal with with Bertie and Mr. High-and-Mighty over there on the hill. Don't know how you're going to get through that grand tour, considering how fond you are of him. Try to resist the temptation to push the man down the basement stairs, will you? Geoff Black said that you have to be . . . what was the word he used? 'Diplomatic.' " Jess's eyes twinkled. I wasn't amused.

"Mrs. Louis," I could hear quiet panic in Geoff Black's voice when he'd called me earlier in the week. "Please don't antagonize Mr. Hayward-Smith. We want to keep things civilized."

"Diplomatic, my butt."

Jess's eyebrows rose.

"Things not going well?"

"If I hear the words, 'Mr. Hayward-Smith would like to

point out . . .' again, I am going to open the basement door
and push them all down the stairs. The man finds one
speck of dust, one that I can't see, and now he wants his
room dusted twice a day. He says he's allergic to the rye
bread we use for his morning toast so he's having some
sent by FedEx from New York City. He doesn't like the
soap we use. He thinks the water is hard and shouldn't we
put in a water softener." I glared at Jess. "Why did they
outlaw drawing and quartering?"

Jess whistled and turned his attention back to the gumbo
in progress.

"Glad it's not me you're mad at."

I watched Jess as he put his meal together but I didn't
really see him because I was thinking so hard. I was mad at
Mr. Pointy Nose High-Up Butt. He's a stuffed shirt with
an Evian bottle up his butt. But it's his attitude about his
mother that really gets to me. He's ready to tear down a
perfectly good old house and sell the land, and he doesn't
even need the money. Geoff Black said he inherited millions from his father and made millions of his own. I think
I'm mad at Hayward-Smith because he's doing all of this
out of meanness, just for spite, to get back at Millie because
she wasn't there when he was growing up. Hayward-Smith
talks about her as if she was a neurotic sex fiend. He makes
me angry when he makes snippy comments about her that
don't sound like the woman I knew at all. I'd like to ask
him where he heard those lies but Geoff has warned me
not to get into a "discussion" with Hayward-Smith. That's
what Geoff calls it, a "discussion." White people discuss
things. Black folks argue. OK, I promise not to discuss anything with Mr. Pointy Nose. But if he pushes me the wrong
way, he's going to get an argument—a big one.

When I told Jess this, he shook his head.

"Did you take your pill today?" he asked, teasing me.

"Not today, probably not tomorrow either," I told him. "May not take them ever again." I was gleeful when I said this. "Those power surges just might be good for something."

Jess turned his eyes heavenward.

Chapter Ten

I took Broderick Hayward-Smith on a top-to-bottom tour of Millie's house. We started in the basement and worked our way up. I should have saved myself the misery and pushed him down the basement steps. The tour was a disaster.

This was a man who hated everything. That's a sign of bad digestion. Every stick of furniture, each dish, and all of the paintings were targets. He didn't miss a chance to talk bad about the house, the Northwestern United States, Paper Moon, Montana, or Millie—especially Millie.

"These furnishings are frightful!" H-Smith exclaimed when we stepped into the back parlor. "Victorian, Art Deco . . ." he waved a hand across the top of a sleek desk that Millie bought just before she got sick. "Modern, Country, French . . . all mixed up together. It's horrible. Couldn't she make up her mind?"

He never called her "my mother" or "Millie" or even "Mrs. Daniels." It was as if Millie didn't deserve a name.

Just said "she" or "her" with nastiness pouring into those words. I wanted to tell him that he could take that attitude and stuff it up his butt along with the Evian bottle but I bit my tongue, remembering what the attorney had told me: "Mrs. Louis, please try to be patient, it's not for much longer."

Funny thing, though. The way the house was furnished never bothered me much, but then, I don't know anything about interior decorating and don't care as long as the room feels good. The parlor was a little eccentric but it was so Millie that you didn't think about it. I tried to shoo Tonio off the Eastlake chair but he sniffed at me and flopped over. Oh, well. But Louis, who'd been snoozing on the sofa, took one look at H-Smith and took off.

H-Smith was standing near the mantel looking up at the picture of his mother, the one that Taubert had painted during their love affair in the late thirties. I wondered what he was thinking. Judging from the constipated expression on his face, it wasn't anything good.

I think my art teacher would call it a "character study." And Millie certainly was a character. The fact that Millie was naked was beside the point of the painting. She was reclining on a chaise, her hips draped with a shawl of some kind, her feet bare. The background was half Chinese screen, half window looking out on a vineyard. Millie looked straight at the painter with a serious expression, her dark-blue eyes (the ones she'd passed along to her son) had a straightforward tilt to them, intelligent eyes. She didn't look like a woman who felt self-conscious about being naked. She didn't even look seductive. She looked like a woman who had chosen to pose for the portrait and didn't have the slightest regret about it. Her dark-brown hair flowed around her shoulders. Her hands were expressive but strong-looking and, unlike most of the photographs of her that I'd seen from that time, Millie's nails weren't painted. I remembered her telling me that she and her husband, the Count, worked side by side in the vineyards and that she'd loved working with her hands. No red nail polish for her in those days.

I heard H-Smith say under his breath, "Libertine."

I wasn't familiar with that word but the way that he said it told me what it meant.

"She was not," I told him.

He glared at me.

"What else would you call a woman who would . . . pose for such a painting?" He stalked out of the room. "My father was right about her . . ."

He tried to find fault with the dining room but there wasn't much he could say. It is a beautiful room, grand and gracious like you'd see in the movies. Millie's English husband gave her the mahogany Chippendale table and matching chairs. They are worth a small fortune by themselves. So, instead, he made a comment about the china pattern she'd chosen.

"It isn't real Havilland," he said with a sniff. "This was made after the War."

Oh, who cares? I thought. *As long as you can eat Cheerios out of it.*

By the time we got to the Mauve Room, I was ready to give the man an enema. He didn't like the Oriental rug in the Violet Room. Obviously, "she" had no taste at all. The draperies in the Merlot Suite were too dark, "her" provinciality was showing. The draperies in the Mauve Room were too light. The chandeliers in the hall needed rewiring, "she" was not one for details and on and on . . .

I was beginning to think of devious ways that I could

hurt this man. I was counting to ten, then twenty, then fifty after most of his snippy comments, just to keep from cursing him out and telling Geoff Black to hell with the whole thing. Then, I unlocked the door to Millie's room. Inez and I had been keeping it locked so that none of the guests would wander in. I think we felt that it was still Millie's personal space and it wasn't right to expose it to other people. The room was pretty much as Millie had left it. I led Hayward-Smith through the sitting room (I didn't mention that Millie had called it her "boudoir") and into the bedroom. We'd had her cherry four-poster bed brought up from the basement. Inez and I made up the bed ourselves, blinking back our tears as we smoothed out the soft lavender-colored sheets, the lace-trimmed pillow shams, and the white chenille spread.

H-Smith didn't have much to say. He walked around and I watched him, waiting to pounce on him when he said something mean about Millie. But he didn't.

That is, he didn't until we got ready to leave.

"That's it, Mr. H-Hayward-Smith. I'll just lock up."

"When this hearing is over, I want this room cleared out, from top to bottom, the draperies, the rugs, her . . . her personal effects, and everything else. Sell them, throw them into the dustbin, or into the lake—I don't give a damn what you do with them. I don't ever want to see them again." He spoke with crisp, razor-sharp enunciation and a lot of anger wrapped around his words like a coat of armor. Hard and cold.

My feet were glued to the floor.

"What are you talking about?" I demanded. Geoff Black's warnings about behaving myself flew right out the window.

"You heard me," he said in a booming voice.

"I heard you all right," I said. "You're just a little early, buddy. This place ain't yours yet."

"I will succeed."

"Yeah, but you might not."

"Then I'll buy you out, Mrs. Louis, and do what I want to do," he countered. "Name your price. I can make it worth your while."

I stared at him. This stuff only happened in movies.

"Oh, yeah? And if I did sell to you? Say for . . ."

He butted in with a number that I only heard when the business segment of the evening news was on.

"Right," I answered, trying not to act stunned. "What if I did? What would you do with Millie's place?"

"Tear it down."

I felt sick.

"I'm sure that you understand that I intend to prevail in this matter. Regardless of what I have to do or what I have to spend. And when I do . . ." he looked around him. His pointy nose had curled on the end and his mouth had turned into a real upside-down smile. His face was so scrunched up that he looked like an albino prune. He looked downright ooglee. "I want this room emptied out. I want every trace of *her* removed . . . or destroyed. Especially . . . especially that pornographic painting in the rear parlor. And I want you . . ."

"Excuse me, Mr. Hayward-Smith," I interrupted him. "In the first place, I am not your employee and I am *not* your servant. You need to take that condescending bullshit to someone who can appreciate it. I can assure you, I am *not* that person. And if you 'prevail,' as you put it, the first damn thing I'm going to do is walk out the front door. Somebody else can do your dirty work."

"I intend to prevail, Mrs. Louis," he repeated.

"Yeah, well, that will be what it is," I told him, moving toward the door. "For all your high-ass knowledge about this antique and that brand of china, you don't know too much, do you?" I gestured toward the furnishings in Millie's bedroom. "Just about every piece of furniture and rug, down to the smallest teacup, was chosen by *your mother* with a lot of thought and care. She traveled all over the world, and she's got books in the library about these things she's collected. I don't know much about Limoges or East Lakes, but *your mother* did. And she cared for these things with a lot of love and enjoyed sharing them with her guests." I glared at him. "Enjoyment seems to be a word that you don't know much about." *Probably because your intestines are in a knot.*

One thing besides the blue eyes that Hayward-Smith inherited from his mother was tenacity. Once Millie Tilson got her teeth into something, whether it was a piece of furniture that she was bidding on at auction, a book that she was reading or a topic that she was arguing about, she never, ever let go. Obviously, her son was cut from the same corduroy.

"I will prevail," he repeated. "And when I do, I will make arrangements to have this room stripped down to the bare walls." He ran his hand along the soft shell-pink wallpaper with its climbing rose-patterned border. "Strip this wallpaper off as well." He might have been talking to me when he said that. He might have been talking to himself.

That's right. Strip Millie clean out of that house. "Rose" was Millie's middle name. She'd chosen the wallpaper for that reason.

I bumped into him—hard—on my way out of the suite,

jiggling the keys in my hand as I went. I had had enough of Mr. High-Up Butt today. If it weren't for the hearing, I would have walked out that door right then and let this jerk change his own hand towels twice a day.

"What's that saying, Mr. Hayward-Smith, 'until the fat lady sings'? Well, she ain't even warmed up, so you just keep your big drawers loose until she does. And, *until* she does, this room stays just like it is, down to the last little Post-it note." The door was open and I pointed toward it. "After you." *Asshole.*

What he said next caught me completely off guard.

"Yes, it does seem that she never threw anything away." He glanced at me as he said this and my breath caught in my throat. It was as if the male version of Millie's face was looking back at me. "Except for me."

He walked past me out into the hall and headed up the back stairs to the Tower Suite. I'd heard Elva Van Roan thumping around up there earlier but she was quiet now. The fax machine beeped a couple of times and then went silent. The only sounds I heard were his large and heavy feet clomping up the narrow steps and the muffled sound of the door closing.

Except for me.

I stood in the middle of Millie's room. Broderick Tilson Hayward-Smith was rich, had degrees from several universities, and had traveled all over the world. His daddy left him a fortune and he was a millionaire himself. He was over sixty years old and still grieving for the mother whom he thought had given him away like a piece of unwanted furniture.

There are talk shows about this and doctors preach to folks over the radio and how many books have been writ-

ten on this subject? I'd heard one serrated-tongued coun-
selor tell an unhappy listener, "Get over it!" And another
on TV telling a sobbing woman to "grow up." But getting
over it and growing up aren't as easy as they sound. And if
the background story was ever told, those doctors have
problems of their own. Hayward-Smith was living proof
that some pain takes a long time to heal, if ever, like over
sixty years.

I found the key to lock the door. Then I saw the folder
on Millie's desk and smiled. The story for her creative
writing class was in that folder. She'd been really pissed off
about getting a "B" on it. "It should have been an A," she
had sniffed indignantly. "All of that feeling, all of that loss,
poured into the story and I get a lousy B!"

All of that loss. I picked up the folder and locked the door
behind me. I had only heard part of the story. Millie was
still working on it that starry summer night. I'd asked her
if the story was fiction. She had looked away, still stroking
Asim, and never really answered.

After this, time just seemed to fly by. My "to-do" lists
were getting longer and longer. I had borrowed the idea
from Millie, who had lists for everything. But now I had
five lists and they each had over ten things on them. My
lists had lives of their own. I was working on the "personal
stuff" list. It was a Thursday, no classes, and I was finished
at the inn for the day, sitting on a stool at the diner. It
was three o'clock in the afternoon, the lunch crowd was
gone—just a few folks having coffee—and dinner was several hours off.

This was the longest list: wash hair, call KayRita, order
hot sauce, no, that goes on the "diner" list. . . . I was still
managing my list when Mountain came in. The cold air

came in with him and rustled the pages of my notebook. As I smoothed them down again, I said "hey" to him and kept scribbling. Heard Mary take his order: half a tuna sandwich, applesauce, child's portion, and Coke. Sighed to myself. That boy was going to waste away to nothing. The last time I'd seen him the collar of his shirt was loose. But there was no talking to Mountain about it. He was still broken up about Lawra and it was going to take time.

The door opened again and my notebook pages flapped. It was still cold around here and I couldn't seem to get my ankles warm, no matter what I wore. But if the front door is opening that means the diner is doing well, so I don't complain. That's good for Jess. I didn't even look up but heard whoever it was stomp the snow off their feet and head toward the counter.

"Ms. Louis?"

It was Amy Hsu, Mr. High-Up Butt's executive assistant. Cold weather did not agree with her. She looked like a very chic Popsicle. Her nose was red and from the way she scrunched up her shoulders, I could tell that she was freezing.

"Amy, you look like you're about ready to turn into ice. You want a hot chocolate? Some tea?"

She smiled; a pretty girl but wrapped a little tight, if you asked me, all business all the time. She moved at the speed of light, buzzing here and there. I wondered if the child had any fun. I guess that came from working with Mr. Personality over there in the Tower Suite.

"Actually, I came over to see if I can get lunch, but hot chocolate sounds terrific," she said, rubbing her hands together. Her lips were so numb that her words sounded funny.

"Sit down, girl, take your coat off. I'll get you a menu and something hot."

I swear I wasn't gone more than thirty seconds. OK, maybe I was gone a whole minute, but no more than that. When I came back, Mountain was draped around that girl like a sausage casing (I *know* how to do sausage casings now), his smile wider than the Grand Canyon, his eyes a color of blue that I hadn't seen since he and Lawra Svenson did the Booty Call at Millie Tilson's funeral cabaret.

"Juanita, this meal's on me," Mountain said, sounding like the last of the big spenders. How much can a small garden salad, cup of tomato soup, and hot chocolate cost? "You never told me that Mr. High-Up Butt, er, Hayward-Smith, had such an exquisite and erudite executive assistant!" He beamed at Amy.

Both Mary and I forgot our manners and stared for a moment. "Exquisite"? "Erudite"? Mountain?

"Sheriff Peters was telling me about the diner's history," Amy said. "It's *so* romantic. How you took over the cooking, and you and Jess fell in love."

Who *was* this woman?

I swear to God, Amy, Miss Sophisticated-Midwestern-meatloaf-wouldn't-touch-my-lips Hsu beamed back at that man as if he was the Apollo of Montana.

"Just call me 'Frank.'" Mountain said in a voice I have never heard him use. And no one, not even his mother, calls him "Frank." "I'm so glad that, of all places, you decided to walk in here."

Mary and I exchanged glances. Like there are that many choices in Paper Moon?

"Oh, well, yes, I guess it's a good story," I managed to stammer as I dropped off the hot chocolate. Neither of them was paying any attention to me at all. "Amy, your soup and salad will be out in a minute," I said to no one in particular.

"Thank you," Amy said. Her eyes never left Mountain.

"Juanita, I think I'll just escort Miss Hsu over here to my table," Mountain said as if he was talking about a reserved table at the Ritz-Carlton. "Oh, and could I put in another order?"

When I gave the slip to Jess, he whistled.

"Good God! When did a family of four come in?"

I chuckled.

"Not a family of four, just Mountain's appetite back from a short leave of absence."

"The boy finally realized he was starving to death?" Jess pulled out a Texas-sized hamburger patty.

"The boy's in love again," I said.

Jess rolled his eyes.

"I'm in love, too, but if I ate like that I'd get too fat for those weird sexual positions that you like." The hamburger hit the grill with a sizzle.

"You are a silly man," I told him.

"Just trying to keep you satisfied while you're back. It's hard being in love with a rolling stone."

"Oh, please. Where's that salad?" I ladled out the tomato soup. While I got Amy's order ready, Jess sang.

Juanita is a rolling stone,
Wherever she lays her hat is her home . . .

"You'd better pay attention to that hamburger because you won't make much of a living on the Temptations Reunion Tour."

By the time I got back to Amy and Mountain, they were ready to order the wedding invitations. I have heard of love at first sight but this is the first time I have seen it with my own eyes.

"I hear that you're having a 'Soul Food Night,' Juanita," Mountain said to me while keeping his eyes glued to Amy as she sipped her soup with ladylike delicacy. "Grits, sweet potato pies, macaroni and cheese, corn pudding . . ." Mountain's face lit up. Just mentioning several starchy foods together gives him a high. "Ribs, fried catfish . . ."

"In three weeks," I told him, wiping my hands on my apron. "No grits, Mountain. I only do them for breakfast mostly."

But Mountain had already moved on.

"That's too long to wait. Miss Hsu, may I take you to dinner next Saturday? Say, seven o'clock?" Amy looked like Cinderella who'd just found out that the glass slipper fit her tootsies. "I think you'll enjoy the meal . . . and are you free tomorrow night, too?"

I didn't stay for her reply, I could guess what it was anyway. Yes, she would marry him; yes, she would have several ten-pound babies with him and, by the way, yes, she'd be happy to go to dinner with him tomorrow night. I glanced outside: snowing again, wind blowing, probably thirty degrees. Yep, it was definitely the season for love.

When I came back into the kitchen, Jess was prepping for dinner and Mary was helping. I was just in the way so I picked up my lists then realized that there was something that I was supposed to do. The problem was, I couldn't remember what that *was*. I didn't have this problem in my old one-dimensional life in Columbus. Of course, I didn't have as much to remember then, either. Now, I needed lists and a calendar to keep up with everything that I was responsible for. So, I had started forgetting things. I would get up and go into the kitchen, forgetting what I was going in there to get. I started leafing through papers, then forget what I was looking for. Of course, I could just be getting old. Scary. So, now I sat at the far end of the counter, shifting through my lists looking for . . . ah! Looking for . . . mail, office supplies list, recipe for corn pudding, hospitality class syllabus, and letter from attorney.

I came across the file folder that had Millie's short story in it. Like most other things, I'd forgotten all about it, just stacked other stuff right on top. I smiled. It was a nice story, at least it was from what I'd heard of it. I hadn't actually read it. I looked up in time to see Mary slicing a piece of pie, Jess and Randolph engrossed in the prep for tonight's dinner shift. Once again I forgot what it was that I was looking for and started reading.

Millie's Story, page eight

Just outside Nairobi, Kenya, Shade Gazelle Farm
Owned by David Hayward-Smith

The little boy toddled toward her, first swaying one way, then another. As his fat, stubby legs became surer of themselves, he picked up speed. Giggling, he staggered over to her, like a happy drunk, his round face radiant with the triumph of moving on his own at last. As he got close to her, he raised his arms to be picked up. His mother swept him into her arms and buried her tear-dampened face into the folds of his neck.

"Mummy . . . stop, Mummy!" He squealed and swatted at her as she kissed him everywhere, especially on the tip of his nose. She hugged him tightly as if the imprint of his little body on hers could be stamped on with a permanent ink.

The man stood in the doorway, tall and dark with

an ominous expression on his face. He looked like the shadow of death and would have been pleased to know it.

"He'll ruin your makeup," he said, simply.

"I don't care," she said, her words muffled by the tears and the kisses she planted on the squirming little boy.

The baby giggled.

"MUMMY!" He pushed at his mother with one fat little arm. He was smiling, his blue eyes, her blue eyes, twinkled with merriment. His mother's heart began to split apart.

"W-what are you going to t-tell him? What will you say when he asks where I am?" she managed to say to the dark presence looming in the doorway.

He took a long drag on his cigarette and blew out the smoke slowly. He made her wait for his answer. Cruelty was a hobby with him.

"I'll tell him that you left. That you didn't want to take him with you."

Her dark-blue eyes blazed as she set the baby down. The little boy toddled away to chase a ball that the cat was batting about.

"But that's not true! I'd never leave him like that! I wanted to take him with me!"

"And bring him up in a speakeasy? Or in the wings of a theater? I think not." His voice boomed. It was cold and hard. She shivered. "Besides, we've settled all that."

"I would make him a good home," she countered even though she wasn't certain.

"Well, now you won't have to worry about that, will you? He'll be perfectly looked after and have a very proper home. Right here." David inhaled deeply again. "And you haven't done too badly for yourself."

The money was enough to keep her in furs, diamonds, and Chanel for a lifetime. It still was not enough for what she had to give up.

She wiped away the tears with one gloved hand.

"I'm going to tell him, you know. Someday. I'll tell him what you did." Her words were defiant but her voice cracked.

David Hayward-Smith was not moved.

"If you say anything, if you ever come near him, I will cut him off completely. He'll be poorer than the poorest rat in London. Do you understand, Rose? I will make him a bastard with the stroke of a pen." David glanced over at his son, now playing with the ball in the sunroom. "I will turn him out of this house like a dismissed stable boy."

Rose looks back on that moment and cringes. She chides herself for her cowardice. She should have had the courage to take the baby with her but what would she have done with a baby in prewar Europe, a woman alone with nothing but her voice and her wit to keep her alive? Could she have kept a child fed and warm on wits? Maybe she should have tried. She thinks of the many times that she watched her son from afar from behind school gates, at cricket matches, and sitting in the back of the cathedral when he graduated Oxford. From beneath designer hats, from behind sunglasses, from the shadows, she watched his life unfold. The school photos that she kept, the newspaper articles that she clipped about his career. Even after David died, she kept her distance as if David's ghost would come back and threaten her again. But by then, of course, there was no point, was there? The son was over sixty years old: He'd lived a lifetime without her. What would he do with an old woman, an eighty-year-old mother whom he'd never met? A mother whom he'd been told had left him behind like last season's swing coat hanging, forgotten, in the back of a closet?

I kept my end of the bargain but it was the hardest bargain I ever made. David became a hero in Kenya. His public face was unblemished. His private one, the face that I knew, was a horror. I had read the accounts about my son's mysterious mother, her name unmentioned, and how she just left in the middle of the night, just disappeared, never writing him a letter or trying to see him. And I had been too afraid to correct the lies. David Hayward-Smith left me no choices. I left darling Broderick with his father so that he would receive his rightful inheritance and carry on the Hayward-Smith name. And now, he has.

Millie was a good writer. She'd said that her creative writing instructor's favorite quote was "No tears in the writer, no tears in the reader." Well, I had to brush tears away so Millie's face must have been soaked.

The sweat rolled down my face from her description of the heat of Kenya and my nose itched from the smell of the animals. I was startled by the sounds of unknown creatures rustling around in the night. And, in the distance, sometimes when the insects weren't too loud, you could hear the lions and the singing and the music, sounding scratchy and falsely high-pitched on the gramophone, instruments that sounded like someone had fashioned them out of tin. I saw the young mother at her dinner party, wiry and vivacious with dark auburn-brown hair, cut and marcelled in the style of the time, a long cigarette holder between her fingers. Her dress was a rich, deep burgundy, "merlot" as Millie had called it, using wine terminology that she'd learned from the Count. In my mind, a sleeveless dress with a dropped waistline trimmed in satin ribbon, fitted over and over again until its wearer was completely satisfied. With the dress, the lady would have worn strapped shoes in leather dyed to match and ropes of perfect pearls around her slender neck. It was a dress designed and stitched by the house of Schiaparelli. I remembered that name. It had taken me several tries before I could pronounce it. It was a beautiful dress and I had seen it myself, carefully preserved, and hanging in a clear garment bag in one of Millie's closets.

A little boy, chubby and outgoing: Did his mother's absence turn him into a stick man with a chip on both his shoulders? I felt the wetness of her tears on the baby's neck and the stonelike heaviness of her chest as she sobbed in the back of the car on the way to the train station. She would not be consoled then. And, from the look on Millie's face that evening when I saw her stroking the secretive Siamese, I don't think she ever was.

I closed the file folder and leaned over the counter. Jess, Randolph, and Mary buzzed around me and wonderful smells floated up from the saucepans and pots on the huge stove. But I wasn't tuned in to that. My mind was far away, over sixty years and a continent-and-a-half away.

Millie had taken a creative writing course but what I'd read wasn't fiction. The pain that seeped out of her words was real. She had loved her son with everything she had, enough to give him up so that he would have the kind of life that she'd wanted him to have but couldn't give him herself. And she had lived all of these years, or seemed to, with joy in her heart, a wild sense of adventure and humor. But all the time, Millie had nursed this wound, this hole in her heart, had stitched it up, bandaged it, covered it up, and masked it with every trick of camouflage that she knew.

But it wasn't enough.

Jess took a sip of the concoction (something French, "cock of" something or other) and winced. I guess the seasoning was off. He grinned at me and waved the spoon around as he looked for the missing ingredient.

I smiled but didn't really see him.

All I saw was a little boy raising his arms upward to a woman who smiled through her tears.

Chapter Eleven

"*I wonder what would have happened if . . .*"

Is that what life comes down to, a basketful of "what ifs"? What if I had done this instead of that? Would life be better or worse? What if Millie had taken her son with her instead of leaving him with David Hayward-Smith? What if I hadn't come to Paper Moon or what if the sun just decided not to rise one morning? And what if you don't have any "what ifs" to choose from?

Sometimes there aren't any choices; someone takes them right out of your hand and you're stuck with what *they* want you to have. Other times you have a lot of choices but none of them are good ones. And you have to make the best of it, as Millie did. As I had to do for years and may have to do again. With Bertie.

She has threatened to fly to Missoula, with Teishia along for the ride. Lord knows where she's going to get the money but Bertie always finds the money to do the things that *she* wants to do. Now she's decided that if I won't come to her then she'll come to me. Bertie is an expert at backing people into corners. She knows that I'll do the right thing for the simple reason that she won't. And Teishia is caught in between.

I hadn't slept well in a string of nights, tossing and turning, twisting this problem around in my head and always coming back to the same answer. Jess and I talked about it until we were both blue in the face. I was anxious and worn down. Jess was easier about this in his mind than I ever would be in mine.

"Aw, don't worry about it," he told me. "I helped my sister with Mignon and Cathy. Little girls are a piece of cake. It's the *boys* that are trouble."

"I feel so helpless. She's going to come, I know it. She'll leave the baby and take off. And I won't see her again for ten years." She was backing me into a cage and I didn't want to go. Bertie was setting me up just like a grifter running a con. I wouldn't have any way to turn but her way. My chest felt heavy. "Jess . . . I love Teishia but I don't want to raise another child."

"What makes you think she'll do that?" Jess asked.

I snorted.

"That's her way. 'See ya later, Ma' and it will be one thing or another. 'Hey, Mom, I'll come and get her in two weeks.' Or, 'the plane ticket went up. I have to wait until the price comes down.' Or, 'I'm working weekend nights to pay off that last AEP bill, just a couple more weeks . . . ' "

"Then tell her *no*," Jess's voice was harsh, a contrast to the soft, warm darkness. I felt him stretch out next to me. It was two in the morning. He yawned. Poor Jess, this was the third time this week that I had awakened him with my restlessness.

A two-letter word with such a complicated meaning. Was it only complicated if you said it and didn't mean it?

"This is not your problem, Jess; it's mine."

"It is when it keeps me up at night," he teased me. He pulled me into his arms. His body was warm and soft and I closed my eyes and tried to think of something else. But Bertie's voice and Teishia's face were the only pictures that moved across my mind; a moving comic strip. "You help me out, I help you out. That's how it works. Now it's my turn."

I shook my head and sighed as I laid my head on his shoulder.

"No. It is definitely my turn," I mumbled.

Jess kissed me.

"Then you'll owe me one," he countered.

But I still couldn't sleep. And then I had a nightmare. I dreamed that I was sitting in a closet-sized room, in a chair wedged between an elephant and a rhinoceros. If I moved, I'd make the elephant mad or spook the rhino. I was stuck.

For the next week, I went through the days with the joy of a person who's waiting for the other shoe to drop—a really big shoe.

School was getting more and more difficult. I'd been staying up late at night, studying, trying to understand the percentages and conversion charts, trying to figure out how to apply this chemistry to baking a simple loaf of bread (that wasn't really simple) or making a croissant. I wasn't doing very well. My croissants were chewy. And my hors d'oeuvres were too big. Chef looked at them then glared at me.

"Madame Louis, I *said* to make them bite-sized. Unless you plan to serve Goliath at your reception, these bowling balls will take the average person four bites to eat."

I was discouraged. We had a big test coming up. I didn't think any number of study-group sessions or all-nighters would help me. I made a decision: If I didn't pass this test, and I mean really pass it with a B or better, I was dropping out of the program. I didn't tell Jess because I knew that he would try to talk me out of it.

Didn't have too much to say to anyone that week. Inez was worried that I was coming down with the flu.

"No, I'm OK," I told her. What is that called when you just want to crawl into bed, pull the covers up over your head, and stay there for a few years? The blues? Well, I had them and I had them bad.

Inez checked my forehead with the back of her hand then shook her head. "You look peaked," she said with authority. "You better take something, lie down awhile. And *stop* moving the furniture and pictures around. Where did you put Millie's portrait?"

"What are you talking about?" I asked her, closing the notebook that I had been using to keep up with the reservations.

"The portrait of Millie. You moved it out of the parlor."

"No, I didn't."

"Well, it's not there."

Sure enough, Millie's portrait, the nude one by Taubert, was gone and a landscape was in its place, one that had been hanging over the washbasin in the Violet Room.

"I didn't move it," I told Inez.

Inez exhaled loudly and looked upward.

"Then we have Elva problems again. I go call the number for the ghost therapist. I found it yesterday in the back of the kitchen junk drawer."

But this wasn't Elva Van Roan's work. She had promised to behave and, unless you got a wedgie over a few thumps and bumps, she had. This was Mr. Pointy Nose High-Up

Butt and I was fed up with him. Until that hearing was held, this was still Millie's house, damn it. And if she'd hung that portrait there, then, by God, there it stayed until the court decided.

I knocked on the door but no one answered so I just walked on in. I found H-Smith in the middle of a business meeting. Amy was tapping away on the laptop, a male voice droned over a speakerphone, and Williams hovered in the background; I wasn't sure exactly what he was doing, but he looked busy.

"Mrs. Louis, we're in the middle of a conference call!" Amy exclaimed.

"Oh, I'm sorry," I said. "I thought you said 'come in.' "

"Mrs. Louis." H-Smith held up one finger. It wasn't his middle finger so I assumed that he was signaling for me to stay quiet for a moment while he finished his call.

"Amory, we have been around this block before. My offer still stands but if it doesn't suit you, then I'll withdraw it. What? I see. Then we have a disagreement in interpretation because I have no interest in adjusting it upward. Now, if you'll excuse me, I have another appointment." He tapped a button and the phone clicked off. Then he turned his attention to me, giving me the same look he always did—as if he was about to squirt me with bug spray. "Mrs. Louis. To what do I owe this unannounced intrusion?"

I ignored the fancy talk. I was too tired to get into word fencing.

"Mr. Hayward-Smith, we agreed that none of your mother's furnishings or personal effects were to be disturbed until after the hearing."

"Yes, that's right," he answered. He was as cool as a

bottle of Boone's Farm that had just come out of the refrigerator.

"Then why did you move your mother's portrait? The one hanging in the back parlor?"

There have been times when I've caught H-Smith off guard and, with his dark-blue eyes, blonde-gray hair, and pointed cheekbones, he looked a lot like his mother, even though I don't think I've ever seen him smile. There are other times, like this one, when his face hardened like concrete into a mask of meanness. I wondered if this was the face of his father, David. It wasn't Millie's face, I can tell you that.

"Yes, I moved it. I won't have it around," he said sharply. "It's disgusting."

"It is not . . ."

"That portrait is . . . filth," he interrupted me, his voice getting louder. The way he said the word "filth" made my stomach turn.

"It is a portrait of *your mother*," I told him. "There's nothing filthy about it."

"She was an irresponsible, promiscuous gold digger and my father was well rid of her."

"You never met the woman. You don't know jack shit about her. She was kind, funny, smart, and generous—"

"Generous with her favors, you mean," he interrupted.

"Generous with her time and her money, generous with her spirit," I told him. "You are a really stupid man, did you know that?"

I thought Mr. High-Up Butt was going to choke. Williams started coughing and quickly left the room with Amy close behind him, her eyebrows raised to her hairline. The door closed with a discreet click.

"You have some . . ."

"Listen here, I have had about enough of this. I love this place, but life is too short to have your head pounding, your stomach churning, and staying up nights wondering what shoe is gonna drop next. The attorney told me to be civil with you but my civility has run out. Your mother, and that's what she was, *your mother*. She was a lady, I don't care what you think."

"I know all that I need to know," H-Smith snapped back. "My father married the woman, he knew all about it . . ."

"I don't care what your jackass daddy thought he knew, he was wrong. Worse than that, he was a liar." If you're going to jump into something, you might as well jump in up to your thighs. Right?

"She was irresponsible and greedy." Hayward-Smith's voice was booming now, a deep baritone that might have sounded good in an opera or something. But now, its tones echoed off the walls of the room and sounded angry, hollow, and cold. "My father paid her off and she took the money like the money-grubbing tart that she was."

"Millie didn't leave you because she wanted to. She left you behind because your daddy told her that he would take away your inheritance if she didn't."

Of course, I couldn't prove that. I only had a short story that might or might not be based on truth to go on, but, what the hell, there was a whole lot in those words that had the ring of truth. And I was now pulling the rope and ringing that huge bell.

I had been fanning myself with the file folder even though it was thirty degrees outside. Now, I just threw it in his face.

"Your momma was a writer, too," I told him. He was too shocked to say anything. "You might want to read one of her stories."

I slammed the door so hard the chandelier swayed from side to side.

I stormed past Inez, grabbed my coat, and trudged down the hill and around the corner to the diner, where I could get something to calm me down.

I don't drink but I sure needed a drink now.

Well, I wasn't going to inherit any bed-and-breakfast. Maybe Hayward-Smith would prove that Millie was nuttier than a fruitcake. I was way past caring. I had just taken care of one of my full plates.

I was so mad that I was practically blind. I was charging along as if it was sixty degrees outside and the walks were clear and dry instead of covered with snow and slush and patches of ice. So, of course, I slipped and fell on my butt. Tried to stand up and slipped again. Good thing I have some extra padding on my backside. By the time I got going again, I was still mad but I was sore, too.

When I walked into the diner, I could tell by the expression on Jess's face that one of my other full plates was about to spill over.

I stomped the snow off my feet and opened the door of the diner. Jess was standing right in front of me.

Do you remember that shoe that I was waiting on? Well, it dropped on my head and flattened me like a pancake.

"Your daughter just called," he said with an expression that would stop a train in its tracks. He paused before he went on, as if he was thinking something over. "She says that Teishia is sick."

Long after I hung up the phone, I just sat there and stared at it.

"Momma, you got to come home . . . 104-degree fever . . . Children's Hospital ER . . . convulsions . . . Momma, I need you . . ."

I heard the sound of a mug sliding across the counter toward me. Hot chocolate, just the way I liked it with more whipped cream than chocolate. But I couldn't drink it. Not now.

"Momma, I need you to come home . . ."

It had not been a nice conversation.

I looked up at Jess, who was filling a tray for a table of cross-country skiers.

"I don't believe her," he said simply as he walked past me.

I said nothing. I didn't believe her either.

Just hearing Bertie's voice, I got a knot in my stomach. Talking with Randy, even with Rashawn, didn't touch me that way. But the sound of my daughter's voice, transmitted loud and clear across the digital microwaves of long distance, came in on a high-quality frequency. And it brought with it more than words. Vocabulary was the runner-up to anger and arrogance and blame, especially blame. The boatload of blame came through just fine and left a sticky, ugly residue of guilt behind as if I hadn't wiped down the counter right. So that when I finished talking (or should I say "listening"?) to Bertie, there was a sharp, sick coldness in my gut as if I'd swallowed Pepto-Bismol laced with sliced razor blades that had just come out of the Deepfreeze.

"She is your granddaughter," Bertie had said, as if she was telling me that two and two were four.

The fingers of my old life were longer and more patient

than I thought. I had figured, after a year or so, they would have given up looking for me, trying to "talk some sense" into me, give up trying to make me come to Jesus and take care of the responsibilities I had to raise my grown children. Like a bank robber from the thirties, I thought I had got away clean.

No way. That old life had tentacles that were long and sticky like a giant squid and they were reaching out to me, grabbing and pulling me back.

Jess slid a thick white envelope toward me.

"What's that?" I was afraid to touch it. I was only getting bad news today.

"Don't know but it's from your favorite person."

HAYWARD-SMITH, INTERNATIONAL LTD.
NEW YORK   SAN FRANCISCO   LONDON   NAIROBI

My already-sinking stomach dropped to my knees. Hayward-Smith and Bertie were tied for my Least Favorite Person Award.

"It's probably a letter bomb," I told Jess. I had no desire to open the envelope—ever.

"Maybe he's withdrawing the will contest."

He wasn't.

Once I got past all the where-asses and fourth-wits, the letter was very clear: Broderick T. Hayward-Smith "was prepared" (boy, that sounded just like him) to pay me a "substantial sum" to deed the inn to him. "Substantial" is a good word. It makes you think of things or people that are sturdy, reliable, conservative. But "substantial" did not come close to the dollar figure that Hayward-Smith was "prepared" to offer. I counted the zeros twice then asked

Jess for his reading glasses. Hayward-Smith was offering enough pennies to buy into Nina's business—three or four times. What could I do with *that* kind of money?

Jess whistled.

"That's a hell of an offer."

According to the letter, I had ten days to make up my mind. Ten days.

I threw my coat over my shoulders, pulled a cigarette from a pack that Peaches had left a hundred years ago, and went out onto the porch. I didn't feel the cold. Jess raised an eyebrow but didn't say anything even though he knew I'd quit smoking. He probably figured that I was having a hot flash and needed to cool off.

Questions, questions, and more questions. Where were the answers?

I looked out across the lake into the north forest where it's green and brown. But spring had put on boxing gloves and was fighting her way into Montana. I heard the voices of birds that I hadn't heard in a while. I wondered, if they're singing to keep warm, that maybe they're thinking they came back too soon. A flash of burgundy from the road, the Ram truck of one of the families that lives farther up the ridge. A roar and the smell of diesel fuel, then silence and clean, cold air.

There is a poem about a road not taken. I think that it's really about the road that *was* taken. I, of course, had never taken any roads anywhere in my life so when my time came, I just picked a road out of the atlas. I was not poetic about it at all. I think the poet was saving the other road for another day. I wasn't sure there'd ever be another road for me. I had only two—the road out and the road back in.

Chapter Twelve

Just like a bad-luck charm, the situation with Bertie brought back everything in my life that I didn't want back, most of the garbage that I thought I had left behind when I caught that Greyhound. All of the anger, the helplessness, and the screaming and fighting. I had fought with each of my ex-husbands, sometimes just yelling and screaming. Sometimes more than that.

I just never thought I'd get into an argument with Jess. At that time, of course, I thought it was a real fight. When the fog finally cleared, I realized that it wasn't. But at that time, I was so upset, confused, and tired that I couldn't tell my head from a hole in the ground.

And Jess, who always seemed to know just what could make me feel good, also had the talent for saying just the right words to make me want to rip his face off.

The bad part about it was, I knew that he was right.

He kept saying it over and over again.

"You're making a mistake."

My jaw was set tighter than the vault doors at Fort Knox. I turned my head away and looked at the few scraggly-looking elk grazing in a field off in the distance. Jess and I had already had this conversation over and over.

I was going back to Columbus and that was that.

"You're making a mistake," Jess said again, louder, as if I hadn't heard him the first time.

"I heard you. And I've said all I'm gonna say. I'm going."

"I think she's puttin' you on, Juanita. I don't think that Teishia's sick. Randy would have called. KayRita would have called. I really think . . ."

"I don't care what you think," I yelled back.

"Little kids get sick, Juanita. You've had three of 'em, you know that," Jess countered.

"Yeah? And you've had none so you don't know anything. They get sick, those fevers spike, what you think is just a little head cold turns into God-knows-what overnight. I've seen it happen. She said T's fever wasn't coming down and she's taking her to Children's. And she said to come and I'm coming. She's my daughter; T's my granddaughter. That is the end of it."

Jess's hands tightened on the wheel.

"What'd your sister say?" he changed direction on me.

KayRita was at a hair show in Cleveland. I finally reached her on her cell phone, screaming in her ear because she was on the main exhibition floor and couldn't hear. She'd told me that she would get her oldest girl, Marlena, to check in with Bertie. Marlena had called me. But the news didn't make me feel good.

"Aunt Juanita? I've called the apartment, Bertie's cell, and Lee's cell. There's no answer. I even went by there. No one's home."

Randy's phone had the voice mail on but I knew that he was out of town, too. He was on a cooking team and there was a competition in New York. I'd talked with him just before he left. He said T was fussy and that her head was a little warm but that she seemed all right and that Bertie wasn't that worried about it. She and Lee had got a sitter and were going out.

"If she's going out, then you don't need to be going out there," Jess said flatly. "She's putting you on, Juanita. She's been calling you for weeks, trying to get you to come back. And now she's finally found the one thing, the bait, if you want to put it that way, that she knows will work like a voodoo spell."

My jaw was so tight that I could feel my teeth grinding into each other until my temples and my jaw hurt. My fists were balled up and my shoulders tightened until it felt as if I had a band of steel across my back climbing toward my ears. I don't like fighting with Jess. Maybe because he doesn't fight dirty. He just tells you what he thinks. No posturing, no mind games, no bring-you-down-on-your-knees remarks, just the truth, whether you see it or not.

For a few seconds, I wouldn't say anything. I couldn't. The thought that Bertie would use her own daughter to manipulate me in this way . . . no, she wouldn't do that. Those other situations? They were small potatoes. But this, this was major, this was hard-core. Bertie was a lot of things: selfish, sometimes lazy, and almost always looking out for her own interests. But I never would think . . . no, I would not admit to myself that that girl would stoop so low. When I could finally speak, I said, "Bertie wouldn't do that." It was all that I could get out because my throat was so tight. I didn't look at Jess when I said it.

We drove the rest of the way to Missoula International without speaking. As we approached the lane for "Departing Flights," Jess said, "Looks like security took the meters out, so I can't park. I'll drop you right here."

"OK," I said. My fingers were wound like steel cord around the handle of my duffel bag.

Jess pulled behind a black Yukon and put the truck in "Park" then got out.

"You don't have to . . ."

The door slammed.

He came around to the curb side and opened the truck door and held my elbow as I stumbled down. I did look at him then. His eyes were even blacker than I remembered, if that was possible.

"When you finish with this nonsense, Miz Louis, you come home, you understand? And if Northwest won't fly you, I'll come and get you."

It wasn't until I felt the lift of the plane in the pit of my stomach that I realized that Jess had said something to me that he'd never said before. On all of my wanderings, he'd always said, "Come back, Juanita," or "Don't forget to come back." And in our conversations, Columbus was always "back home." But not this time.

This time, he'd said, "You come home."

After I'd waited an hour for Bertie to pick me up from the airport, I began to wonder if Jess wasn't right.

"I'll pick you up, Momma," she'd told me in a message she left on the answering machine. "Just tell me what time." We'd played phone tag but I had left her a message with that information.

But she wasn't there.

So I took a cab and watched the flags of many countries flapping in the wind as the car made its way down

Port Columbus International Boulevard. There were so
many new buildings built since I'd left; even the McDonald's looked different! The airport had been built up, of
course, although even when I lived in Columbus, I was
hardly ever at the airport. I mean, when was I ever going
anywhere? The cab turned onto I-670 and the skyline of
the city came into view. Despite the fact that I was as mad
as a hornet because Bertie hadn't been there to meet me
and worried sick to my stomach over what might be
wrong with Teishia, I smiled. The county jail, the Nation-
wide Center, the bank building that looked like a granite
tombstone, the monolithic state office tower: All of those
buildings stood like fortresses from future time, their
squared-off tops disappearing into the haze of the early
spring day. And there, off to the side, dwarfed by the cold-
looking, glitter-and-glass wonders, stood the little Leveque
Tower, the tallest building I'd ever seen when I was a kid.
And, now, its gargoyles and Art Deco curlicues sneered at
accountants on the sixteenth floor of this building or
lawyers on the twenty-first floor of that one.

The cabdriver let me off in front of the apartment and
his tires peeled as he left the driveway. I still had my key.
And it still worked. But I barely recognized the place I'd
left over a year ago.

For one thing, it was clean. Not what I would have expected from my daughter, who was never going to win a
happy homemaker award. And yet, what could I say? The
apartment was neat. For another, it had been completely
redecorated. There was a wall full of sleek silver-and-black
sound equipment and a television large enough to carry a
family of four down the Scioto River on a Sunday afternoon. The couch was new, the end tables were new, and

the kitchen (Lord Almighty!) was spotless. Then I had another thought: Maybe Bertie had moved and they hadn't changed the locks? But, no, there were pictures of Teishia on the shelf next to one of the black electronic what-chamacallits, and some of my pictures were still on the walls.

But the apartment was empty. The bed was made in my old room, and the room that Rashawn had used, Bertie had given over to T because it was furnished with a pretty white daybed and a toy box of stuffed animals set in the corner.

And no one was there. No notes on the refrigerator. No messages blinking on the answering machine. Had I missed her? No. I had called her cell phone. Only the voice mail. I had called her boyfriend. Only the voice mail. With shaking fingers, I punched out the number for Children's Hospital but the friendly voice on the other end informed me that, "for privacy reasons," she could tell me if Teishia was not there, but she wouldn't be able to give me much information if she was. "No Teishia Jackson, ma'am."

Well, that was a relief. Or was it?

I heard Jess's words in my head again: "She's putting you on . . . it's all a head game."

Like I always do now when I need to sort things out, I took a walk. But this time, I wasn't able to charge up a mountain road or meander down a path and look at a Montana lake. I put my bag and my purse in the back bedroom and headed out the door and down Mount Vernon Avenue. It was April, it was a little chilly, but the sun had come out and, as long as I kept moving, I didn't feel cold. Shoot, I'd just come from a state that wouldn't come out from under winter for another month. What was forty-five degrees to me?

Champion Middle School; it was junior high when I went. Union Grove Baptist, Reverend Hale's church, the old Beatty Rec Center. I walked as far as where the old folks' home used to be; what was it called? Looked at the skyline that had changed and the new houses, the marquee lights blinking brightly in the sunlight: the Lincoln Theatre and the old Knights of Pythias Hall—not old anymore—was now the King Center. The more I walked, the more I noticed what had changed. The more I walked, the more I noticed what had stayed the same. And, through it all, even though the memories came back, pushing, shoving, and sometimes, kicking their way into my brain, I didn't feel homesick. I was able, without feeling bad, to remember my smiles as I jumped double-dutch with my friends when I was twelve. I was able to remember the apple crisp that we ate in the cafeteria at Champion; the black and orange of the cheerleaders' uniforms going up and down at the football games at East; my joy when Rashawn was born at old St. Ann's Hospital; the pain when I had my jaw set in the ER room at Grant. The little baby that I'd buried in Evergreen. It all came back, but as I walked back to the apartment, this time on Long Street, I didn't feel sad about it. I didn't feel like I had made a mistake. I thought that I had come back because of Bertie and because I thought Teishia was sick. But maybe, I also came back for me. You know me, I'm a slow learner, and it almost always takes me one more go-round before I catch on.

Bertie walked into the apartment at four o'clock that afternoon with an armful of sacks with logos from Lazarus and Kohl's and Target. She didn't seem surprised to see me. Teishia toddled in behind her, gave a big squeal, and ran into my arms, her legs now sturdy and straight.

Teishia, I recognized right away; I'd seen pictures. Boy, they do grow a lot when they're little. She'd been a big toddler when I left. Now she was more like a little kid. She was acting shy, stuck her finger in her mouth and stared at me with huge dark eyes. As I scooped her up into my arms, she squirmed and tried to get away but I saw a tiny, half smile out of the corner of my eye. Then, she giggled and melted into me, wrapping her little arms around my neck as tight as she could.

"What's my name, what's my name?" I asked her as I kissed her cheek. "What's my name, Teishia?"

"Nana," Teishia said, clear as a bell.

I nuzzled that baby's neck and smelled the sweet soft smell of baby powder. T giggled and shook her head from side to side and my face was lightly pelted with little taps from barrettes that looked like pink elephants, yellow ducklings, and green doggies.

"Nana, you home," she said, still giggling. "Stop, Nana! Wet!" I'll admit it, I can't help it. I did lick the tip of her little earlobe.

"Hi, Momma."

"Bertie," I said to my daughter. It was really all that I could say, mainly because I was so pissed at her that I could hardly say anything decent in front of the baby and because, if I hadn't known who she was, I wouldn't have recognized her. She had slimmed down just like Randy had said, dressed like she was doing a Gap commercial. Her hair was cut short (it was real cute) and she'd cut off the one-inch-long nails, usually airbrushed with blue swirls, that she used to get done bootleg by a girl in the next building. Actually, she was a nice-looking girl. Scowl and all.

"I thought that you were going to pick me up at the airport," I said in a calm voice. "That's what you said in your message." I was counting to myself already to keep from losing my temper.

My daughter shrugged her now-sleek shoulders and set her packages down on the love seat.

"Sorry, I was running late from the beauty parlor and I had to pick up T . . ."

"And go to . . . ah . . . Kohl's and Lazarus and Target and . . . oh! Express. . . . Did you get by the pharmacy to pick up the prescription of amoxicillin for the baby? What about more Tylenol for her fever?" I nuzzled the child again, then let her go. Then I shrugged my shoulders. "No, why would you need to pick up more Tylenol? She doesn't have a fever. In fact, she doesn't seem sick at all."

Bertie looked at me for a split second, then headed into the kitchen.

"She had a one-hundred-and-two fever overnight . . ."

"Over which night, Bertie?" I interrupted her and stood up. T grabbed something yellow, red, and blue out of a bag and ran down the hall to her room chattering to herself. "Over a night last week? Or was it the week before? Just when was it that you had to take this child to the ER? Yesterday? Over the weekend when you got the babysitter and went out?"

Bertie cracked her gum and put her hands on her hips.

"Look, Momma, I did what I had to. I told you months ago that I need you here, home where you belong, to help me with my life. I need somebody to keep T for me. You wouldn't come. Acting like you lost your mind out there in

Wyoming or wherever the shit you are. Probably got bears out there, too. Even Aunt KayRita said you needed to come to your senses."

I knew what my sister had said. I remember it distinctly.

"Girl, you need to come to your senses," KayRita had advised me, and I'd heard the sound of water in the background, probably washing out her customer's perm. My sister laughed, a deep, husky chuckle that sounded like a richly seasoned stew of a few Scotch and waters once or twice a week, Kool cigarettes, one husband, two long-term boyfriends, two grown children, and three grand-babies. She had laughed and told her customer, "Just hold that towel right there, sweetie, I'll be right back. Juanita, you still there? You hear me? I'm telling you, you got to come to your senses. But don't do it too soon, girl! You might as well enjoy yourself while you've done lost your mind." And then she laughed again. "I know I would."

I stretched as far as I could, then reached down to fold the afghan that I'd used to cover myself. Figured I'd counted long enough. I was up to one hundred something.

"I wish that I could say that I can't believe you would use your own child like that, to blackmail somebody, to manipulate somebody into doing what you want. I wish I could say that, Bertie, but I can believe it and I do believe it." I dropped the folded afghan on the couch. "I'm staying the night. I want to play with Teishia a little bit, take pictures of her. And then tomorrow? You're taking me to the airport and I'm catching the first plane back to Minneapolis and, from there, I'm going back to Missoula. Don't pull this stunt on me again."

"Some mother you are," she spat at me, her eyes dark with hatred.

Her anger made me feel sick. The venom in her voice and the heat of her eyes made my head hurt. No, it made my heart hurt. But that's the way it is. You can give birth to them but how they turn out ain't up to you. Sometimes they take their own path.

"I do the best I can, Bertie. There's a story about folks who cry wolf, Bertie. Don't you remember it?"

"Momma, what the hell are you talking about? What do those damn stories have to do with anything? You still got your head in the clouds, just like Rashawn said. Still talking nonsense and bullshit. Still a selfish bitch."

"Yes, I am a bitch," I told my daughter in a voice I knew that she'd never heard before, walking toward her with a step that made her back up until she bumped into the kitchen counter. "I am a bitch. And this bitch is going back to Montana."

I got hooked on reading quotations when I was in Arizona, reading all the brilliant things folks have said over the years. Some man said that you can never go home again. I don't believe that. I think that you can go home again, but you won't be the same person that you were. If you're all right with that, then go on home. But you got to be careful. Nothing stays the same.

Beryl Markham flew airplanes over Africa, and when she left the continent, she really never left. She always carried it in her heart. When she came back, it wasn't the same place, and she wasn't the same woman. I got the feeling, reading her words, that she never got over that disappointment. What she said about life's lessons and being a slow learner, I think, applies to me, too. When you leave a place, especially somewhere that you've been awhile and have a lot of memories of, you can't be wishy-washy about it. You have to get up, pack your bags, and get out. And stay out. And face the new day like you've got some sense. The old days are gone and wondering what went wrong or right won't help. You've got to get on with it.

That sounds like something Millie would have said.

Chapter Thirteen

I left Columbus on a Northwest flight back to Missoula, Montana, by way of Minneapolis. Bertie took me to the airport in her boyfriend's car. At least we were on speaking terms by the time I left.

I said, "Good-bye, Bertie. Thanks for the ride."

She said, "Yeah."

Teishia gave me a hug and a big wet kiss and said "Bye-bye, Nana!"

The romance novels that I read are neat little packages of imaginary lives filled with drama, sex, intrigue, sex, betrayal, redemption, and more sex. All of the loose ends are pulled together in the end, the wrinkles of disappointments and tragedies ironed out on a setting of permanent press with a little steam added for the tough times. Once the bow is tied, the words "The End" appear and you close the book satisfied that everything in the world is OK.

But real lives are not like that; I guess that's why we read these books. I wish that I could tie up my relationship with my daughter with a big, bright pink bow. Sometimes we have the right answers to the questions. Sometimes we don't. And sometimes, we can't tell one from the other.

Jess and I drove back to Paper Moon on a nearly empty highway and in near silence. Occasionally an eighteen-wheeler roared past or a pickup or an old, beat-up car that didn't look as if it should have been able to travel at eighty miles an hour. I saw an elk cow and her calf not too far away and curious cattle grazing near the road. It was still cold and the snow that's come in and out of the hills for the past month still covered the ground in some places, but Montana was shrugging her shoulders, as if she could shake off the winter like a woman taking off a sweater. The smell of ice in the air was gone, replaced by a clean, crisp fragrance. It's the smell of warmth. A funny thing to say since there wasn't any heat attached. But if warmth and spring and renewal had a smell, this would have been it. The sky was blue today, the sun was shining, more boldly than it usually did as if it, too, was telling winter to get lost.

I looked across the plains and the hills and saw the mountains coming closer and closer, more green and brown now than brown and gray. Rough in places, cold and treacherous in places but still beautiful. Like life. Not easy, usually hard, only sometimes smooth, but always, always beautiful.

Living with those rough spots is the hardest part. They fester like sores, they scratch like insect bites, they rub like a sore heel against the back of a shoe. They stick with us; it's a test. Can you still smile and love and rejoice even though you have a sore rubbing against the back of your foot? Can you? Can I?

The layover in Minneapolis had stretched out from one hour to four so we didn't get back to Paper Moon until most of the lights were out in the county. With Randolph manning the kitchen these days, Jess had more time to be my "private chauffeur," as he called it, and I was glad. We spent too little time together; funny thing since we lived in such a small town. I spent most of my days and a few of my nights at Millie's, but most of my nights at Jess's. It just seemed to work out that way.

But now, now the door to "back home" was closing. The probate hearing was coming up. Decisions would be made that I would have to deal with. I didn't know if I was ready or not. Pros and cons, the right thing to do against the smart thing to do, the selfless choice versus the selfish one. Hayward-Smith's offer, school, Arizona, a business of my own . . . the future was hiding in the fog, and I wasn't sure that I wanted it to clear.

I hung up my coat and grabbed my purse, heading down the hall only to find Jess blocking the bedroom door. He pointed to the second bedroom at the end of the hall.

"Got something to show you. It's a surprise," he said, slipping past me toward the other room. He opened the door. "After you."

Dracula got up and loped along beside me.

"Now, what you gonna show me in there but some stacks of boxes, junk from *way* back in the day, including an eight track, I might add, and old clothes?" I teased him.

The extra bedroom was a joke between us. Jess had owned the cabin for over ten years and hadn't unpacked yet. Everything he'd brought with him from his travels and from his life—from Bangkok, Paris, L.A., Vancouver, and St. Louis, or anything he didn't feel like dealing with, like his army stuff—were thrown into that second bedroom. It was filled from ceiling to floor, from window to door with junk. I'd only been in there once. Opened the door and was almost crushed to death by a tower of badly stacked boxes that fell over on me.

I stopped just short of the doorway.

"You mean, you cleaned it out?" I asked him, amazed. "Finally?" Dracula walked past me into the room.

Jess's eyes twinkled.

"It's even better than that," he said.

I walked in and just stood there staring.

All of the boxes and the junk were gone. The eight track was gone, too, and the bits and pieces and parts and portions of gadgets that he'd collected over the years and the five boxes of record albums had disappeared. With the room cleared, I noticed that the floor was hardwood. It had been polished to a shiny golden color and was now partly covered by the Navaho-style rug that I'd bought in Phoenix. Against the south wall was a small futon that Jess had covered with quilts, and a table with a lamp. He'd stacked some of my books there. A small, antique-looking desk sat in front of the east-facing window, and the easel that I'd been using for my art class was set up in front of the south window that overlooked Kaylin's Ridge. He'd taken down the tired-looking canvaslike curtains that I hated and replaced them with white shutters. The baskets that I'd started collecting—sweet grass, Cherokee, and others—sat on the little bookcase next to the door, and my four African violets, rescued from the noise and smoke of the diner, sat serenely in the window.

For once, I was speechless.

And Jess was so pleased that he couldn't stand it.

"I . . . thought you might want a room of your own," he said quietly. "For when you came . . . back. Do you like it?"

Dracula had already made up his mind. He gave me a look that said, "I hope you don't mind but I'm just going to try out this sofa here," as he hopped up on the quilts and settled his large head on the armrest.

I still couldn't say anything. I just walked over to the bookshelf. All of my books were there. I made myself busy by fiddling with the easel, trying to straighten it when it didn't need straightening. Busywork. I ran my fingertips across the top of the little desk where Jess had set a beautiful clothbound notebook and a real elegant-looking midnight-blue ballpoint pen. Perfect. I wiped a tear away with the back of my hand. My African violets—"the quads," as Mignon had named them—were thriving. They had been watered recently and their purple blooms nestled into the deep green furry leaves like a child wrapped in her favorite blanket as she took a nap.

"Jess, I . . ." I looked at him as he stood in the doorway. He was waiting for me to say something definite. And my words were stuck in my throat like crumbled saltines. I knew that my eyes were wet. I opened my mouth but nothing came out.

"This is news," Jess said, his voice gentle. "Wait'll I tell *The County Register.* Juanita Louis is speechless." He was smiling at me but I could tell that he wanted to hear my reaction. The problem was, I was too choked up to say anything. "I . . . you . . . well, Juanita, you don't have to feel obligated or anything. I just thought . . . you might want some space of your own. You know, for when you're here. Instead of half your stuff at Millie's, half here, and all of those boxes that Randy sent and . . ." He stopped and looked at me, his smile fading. "Damn it, Juanita, say something!"

I think I hugged that man so hard that I bruised him. I got the collar of his shirt and some of his hair wet with my tears. He had to hand me a tissue right quick because I almost blew my nose on his sleeve. And I still hadn't said anything coherent.

"I've never had . . ." My throat had squeezed shut and my mouth was just opening and closing. I wanted to tell Jess: *No one has ever done anything like this for me! I've never had a real room of my own, not like this. With just my books and a little place to write and my own couch and . . . never. No one had ever done that for me. And I hadn't gotten around to doing it for myself.* I wanted to tell him that and much more. But none of those words came out of my mouth.

Jess stroked my hair and held my face in his hands and kissed my forehead.

"Just say 'thank-you,' Juanita," he murmured.

"Thank-you." I managed to get those two words out.

"That's OK, Miz Louis," Jess said. "Welcome home."

Depending on how you looked at it, "Soul Food Night" at the Paper Moon Diner was either a big success or a sorry failure. It depended on where you sat, with whom, and whether you got there early or not—because we actually ran out of food. That's a first for the Paper Moon Diner. One thing was for sure, I never thought that those folks who'd lived on brown and white food all of their lives would take to greens, yams, corn bread, and fried fish like they did. As Fats Waller said, "One never knows, *do one?*"

"So what do we have on the menu?" Jess asked. After I told him, he raised his eyebrows. "My cholesterol shot up just listening to you. Is *everything* going to be fried?"

Jess and I had been planning this for weeks. Winter was pretty much over. Folks were getting tired of chilies, soups, and stews, and were ready for spring and sun and flowers and something different to eat. I'd never intruded on Jess's dinner menus (Well, OK, I did intrude *once* . . . those shitty, um, shitake mushrooms.) but he was in an experimental mood and wanted to start hosting "theme" dinners. I warned him not to get too suddity with those.

He'd frowned at me.

"Suddity?" he'd repeated, his forehead dissolving into folds of confusion.

"Jess, these people don't like a lot of frills and fuss," I went on. "Just plain basic food that they can recognize the names of. They want to be able to at least have heard of what you're serving on the menu."

"OK, I'll give you that," Jess answered. "But what's 'suddity'?"

Long-distance phone calls and e-mails to my son Randy helped "refine" the menus. "Refine" was the word that Randy used.

"That kid has a gift," Jess said, printing a recipe that Randy had sent over. "Thinking about getting him out here to help me overhaul the dinner menus, maybe in July. Maybe August. Do you think he'd come?"

I was prouder than I could say. My boy, the chef, was refining menus. And maybe someday, if I passed this next big exam, I might be doing the same thing. Maybe here in Paper Moon, maybe in Sedona. Hayward-Smith's offer briefly cast a shadow across my thoughts. If I accepted, I could buy two inns and have change left over. I'd have enough cash to do a lot of things for a lot of people. But Millie's legacy would be paved over and used as a parking lot.

If I didn't take Mr. High-Up Butt's offer, I could try to make a go of the inn. There was a little money left to run it but not enough for much of a cushion. If the business didn't take off, I would have to close Millie's and sell out anyway. And I'd be right back where I'd started. I tried to focus my thoughts but the loose ends of my life zipped around my head like racing cars.

School was making me feel stupider by the day. My "make or break test" was coming up. I had made up my mind that if I got a C-plus or better on the test, I would see it through to graduation next spring. If I didn't, I was out of there. It's not that I wanted to fail, it wasn't that at all. But I had begun to wonder if I was cut out for the program. The "schoolwork" part was pretty tough on me. Plus, I had to get really used to being on my feet twelve hours a day instead of six. I was, after all, just about the only person in the class over the age of fourteen. The other students were nice, and the ones on my cooking "team" were great, especially the redheaded kid, Marc, who was my biggest fan. But I was still in over my head with the homework and the conversions and trying to figure out how to adapt the formulas to make two loaves instead of three or three dozen éclairs instead of four dozen. It didn't help that I felt that I was the least "decorated" student in the class. Just hearing some of the others talk about their engineering exploits and chemical experiments, spreadsheets and business projects made me blue. I only had a degree in the school of very hard knocks. So I was already practicing my "I've dropped out" speech—the one I was going to deliver to Jess.

The bed-and-breakfast was running nicely (Thank God for Inez!) but Hayward-Smith and I weren't speaking. It was a diplomatic freeze. He sent messages to me through

Williams or Amy Hsu. I saw him a couple of times when I was working at Millie's but he didn't speak. And I didn't either. The hearing, now only two weeks away, couldn't come soon enough for both of us. And I had four days left on his offer. After my trip back to Ohio, I was just a bit frazzled. That was when Jess reminded me that I was directing the next theme dinner.

"It was your idea, y'know," he said.

Great. Another self-inflicted wound.

The Sonoma Valley wine night (my idea) was a hit with the up-and-comings from Missoula, the northern Italian night (Jess's idea) was a complete sellout, we even had folks eating in the kitchen! Capacity for the diner is sixty and there were at least seventy-five people there, but since the fire chief was sitting at the counter, marinara sauce dripping down his chin, we got off easy.

"Soul Food Night" was scheduled just at the time that every other damn soap opera in my life started boiling over. So when Carl backed up the truck on Friday and began carrying in boxes of fish, fresh chickens, cans of condensed milk for the sweet potato pies and, not to be overlooked, brown paper sacks full of collard greens, I was, as they used to say in my great-grandmother's day, "in a state."

"Is this some kind of Italian lettuce?" Carl had asked, holding up one elephant ear–sized leaf. " 'Cause if it is," he added, flicking at something with his fingers, "there's a spider sleeping on the underside." The arachnid fell to the floor and started to make an escape but was stopped by the heel of a size ten-and-a-half Timberland boot.

"Of course," I told him, trying to keep my composure as the food was being brought in. There was so much of it!

"No self-respecting bunch of collard greens would be worth any money at all without a few spiders, some mud, and a lot of grit. That adds to the flavor."

Carl looked at me doubtfully and finished putting the sacks on the counter.

"I see," he said. He didn't know whether to believe me or not. These were the first collard greens he'd ever put his eyes on.

I hadn't slept much the night before and my stomach was jumpy. I'd had too much coffee but it didn't work. I was so tired that I was afraid to stop moving in case I fell asleep standing up. Williams had trotted over with another request for Mr. High-Up Butt and I was frustrated because I couldn't get the hang of the percentage conversions that would be on the test. So as I watched the boxes of food pile up, something close to panic set in.

What was I thinking—agreeing to cook for God knows how many people on Saturday night the weekend before an exam? I needed to have my head examined.

But, you know, cooking is not only a job; it is my passion. I can work on meals for hours—chopping, browning, stirring, and frying—and forget about the time. I sing while I cook, I talk on the phone, I joke with Jess, I listen to Mignon's latest romantic drama, and the food simmers on. I am like a painter, only the pots, pans, and plates are my canvases.

This time was no different. Once I got started, I forgot about everything else and felt just fine.

I grabbed up a sack of collard greens and began to pull out the bunches so that they could get washed. Another little spider saw its chance to get away but I got him. Dumped the greens into the sink and started washing. One of the bunches was tied up with a white twist that read "Putnam County, Georgia." That was where my mother had been born. I smiled, remembering her soft, gentle accent and spirited yet ladylike manner. And time flew from there.

"Are we feeding the Jolly Green Giant?" Jess asked in dismay. Every available inch of counter space was full of food.

"No," I answered him, giving the gravy one last stir. "But Mountain's family is coming. Does that count?"

That seemed to pacify Jess. Mountain's family would make the Jolly Green Giant look like he shopped in the petite department. The menu was brown, white, green, orange, and warm all over. There was fried chicken, mashed potatoes, gravy, and green beans cooked with jowl. The collard greens simmered gently in a pot large enough for me to take a bath in, and I'd seasoned them with Kentucky ham hocks the size of the state of Montana itself. A delicate corn pudding sat on the counter, cooling, and the sweet potato pies were hidden because Carl had threatened to steal one. There was macaroni salad (just a little tease for spring), cole slaw, peach cobbler, and, of course, fried perch and catfish.

"I don't eat bottom-feeders," Jess told me as he sniffed at them. When he thought I wasn't looking, he tore off a tiny piece and stuffed it into his mouth.

I swatted him away.

"Then get your pointed nose out of there and *don't* drop boogers on them," I said. "Besides, genius, these are farm raised."

There was a simple yellow cake with chocolate icing, and apple crisp, just like the kind I'd had at Champion Junior High School when I was a kid.

We opened the doors at five-thirty as usual and by eight o'clock, there was hardly a crumb of corn bread left.

Jess had called in the troops—Mary, Mignon, Carl, and even Randolph—to serve dinner. It's a good thing. I think that half the town was there, and folks from Mason, plus my whole team from cooking school. Marc didn't stop grinning the whole time he was shoveling greens into his mouth. And there's something else that I noticed.

I'm going to stick my neck out on this one. Sopping is an art. You either know how to do it, or you don't. I was raised by Southern parents so we know how to sop even though Mother said it wasn't polite. Daddy ignored her and sopped anyway. Sopping is the art of taking a piece of bread, preferably a biscuit or a roll, and scooping up the juices on your plate, whether gravy, butter, or pot liquor. (Don't tell me you don't know what pot liquor is because I do not have time to explain that right now.) I happen to think that this is an art form. New Englanders, Midwesterners (unless they have Southern roots), and people from other parts of the country just don't do it right. We won't even talk about Californians. There's no little finger in the air, no theatrics, or fancy finger work. You hold that piece of baked carbohydrate in your paws and scoop up the liquid with meaningful hand motions. You can't be wimpy about it and you can't put on airs doing it. Like I've said, I always felt that Southern folks knew how to sop; it's in their blood.

But now, I think I'm wrong about that.

You should have seen Mountain sopping up the chicken gravy, and Mr. Ohlson did everything but put his face in the plate to get the last bit of pot liquor from the greens. The others didn't do too badly either, even Amy Hsu and her New York City self. That girl is the size of a Barbie doll but, I'll tell you what, there wasn't a drop of gravy left on her plate when she got done sopping it up with her corn bread. I went over to compliment her personally. She's good. Sopping with corn bread is not easy.

By eight-thirty, Jess went to lock the doors. We were just about out of food! Williams managed to slip in just as Jess started to turn the key.

I was standing over at Mountain's table. (He has a table now.) He and Amy were wrapped around each other like always and I was teasing them about picking out the babies' names before there was a wedding. I knew I was in trouble when they asked me, with serious expressions, what I thought of the names "Taylor," "Tricia," "Thomas," and "Spring."

The place was noisy but Williams is an expert at adjusting the volume when he clears his throat. I heard him. He was standing right at my elbow.

"Yes, Mr., er, Williams?" I could not get the hang of calling him by just his last name.

"Mrs. Louis, ma'am," Williams said solemnly, his eyes darting around the diner at the chomping jaws. "Mr. Hayward-Smith has asked me to pick up a dinner for him. His finance meeting went long. May I see your menu?"

I was having so much fun that I didn't suppress a smile. Shrugged my shoulders.

"Sorry, Mr. Williams, our menu is done for the day. We're just about out of everything. There's not much of a choice now. Wish you hadn't waited so long."

I could tell that Williams was practically starving to death. The hungry look he had on his face told me that the super-sized cup of black coffee he'd gulped down this morning was the only nutrition he'd had all day.

"I see . . . well . . ."

"Have *you* eaten, Mr. Williams?"

I thought I saw the man blush.

"Er, no, ma'am," he answered.

I wiped my hands on my apron, excused myself from Amy and Mountain, and headed toward the kitchen.

"Have a seat, Mr. Williams, I'll see what I can scrape up from the bottom of a pot. For you and for Mr. High-Up Butt."

"Ma'am?"

I heard Jess chuckle behind me.

"Don't have much. Just catfish and collard greens, I hope that's OK?"

Mr. Williams looked panic-stricken when I said that. Probably never had a collard green in his life. But when he finished eating twenty minutes later, I knew that catfish and collard greens were just fine with him. After the first few bites, he abandoned the prissy way he had of dabbing his mouth, tucked the white napkin under his stiffly starched collared chin, and dug in, face first! I didn't realize that such a skinny man could eat so much, so *fast*. I even heard him burp. Well, belch.

His normally waxy-looking face reddened. And then he smiled. He doesn't look as much like Dracula's uncle when he smiles.

"Oh! Excuse me, Mrs. Louis," he said, embarrassed.

I might be wrong but I think that when I had my back turned, Mr. Williams licked his plate clean. There wasn't a spot on it. Talk about Jack Sprat.

We sent him off into the cold Montana night with a plate for Mr. Pointy-Nose High-Up Butt: catfish, collard greens, corn pudding, and three rolls. And one slice of sweet potato pie for dessert.

Jess and I watched him trudge down the walkway into

the parking lot, where one of Mr. High-Up Butt's black-on-black Suburbans was waiting.

I turned over the "Open" sign and Jess and I headed back to our guests. The diner was still three-quarters full.

"Juanita?" I was headed to the counter to get a glass of water while I could still take a minute. I turned around.

"What?"

Jess had a sly smile on his face that was threatening to break into a huge Kool Aid–sized grin.

He paused for a second then he spoke.

"You didn't put anything in Hayward-Smith's food. . . . Did you?"

I beamed at him.

"Humph!" I snapped my fingers. "I'm glad you mentioned that! I must call Inez and remind her to put more toilet paper in the bathrooms. We were a little short the last time that I was there."

Jess's eyes rolled upward.

"Heaven help us," he said, grinning.

"No, darling. Pepto-Bismol, not heaven," I said.

Chapter Fourteen

I never in my life have pulled an "all-nighter." Now, I've stayed *up* all night, I have definitely stayed *out* all night, but I have never, *ever* been fully conscious and sober from sundown to sunup *and* spent the time studying.

There is a first time for everything.

"Hey, Juanita! Study session at my place tonight. Wanna come?" It was Marc. "I can quiz you, you can quiz me, and we can get Olympia to help with the conversion tables. Larry Barrymore and Karen are going, too."

Olympia was the "girl" who had an engineering degree. It was probably a good idea to have her help but just being in the same room with her made me feel dumber than a basket of boulders.

"Aw, she's OK," Marc assured me. "It's not like she smacks your face with it or anything." A small frown flickered across his forehead. "Not often, anyway."

I studied with the "kids" until midnight, drove back to the cabin in Jess's truck, and went to bed. I tried to go to sleep but my eyelids wouldn't close and my brain wouldn't turn off. I felt like a VCR stuck in eternal fast-forward.

Well, shoot, if I'm going to be up, I might as well be studying, I grumbled to myself as I slid out of the warm bed and into the cold darkness of the room. Shivering, I put on my robe, and then put on Jess's robe, too. With my head scarf and thick wool knit socks, I know that I was quite a sight.

"You talking to me?" Jess's voice came from beneath the covers. He wasn't awake, just repeating De Niro's lines from a movie.

"No. Go back to sleep," I told him.

"Hold on to your matchbooks, fellas, it's going to be a bumpy ride."

Jess makes no sense at all when he talks in his sleep—just misquotes lines from movies that he's seen. Somehow he'd mixed up *Taxi Driver* with *All About Eve.*

I headed to the back bedroom and clicked on the light. Dracula raised his big head and opened one eye.

"You go back to sleep, too," I told the dog, sighing. My brontosaurus-sized charcuterie textbook was open. The print was the size of a microbe but it came into focus when I slipped Jess's reading glasses onto my nose. I was the only student in the class who needed reading glasses. Just one more reminder that I was probably too damn old to be staying up all night—partying, studying, or anything else.

Am I too old?

Is that the question or the answer? my conscience asked.

I studied until my head was too heavy to hold up anymore. Napped for an hour, got up, showered, and got ready to go to school. I still felt dumber than a basket of boulders. But there was no turning back now.

"Whoa! You look wrecked!" Marc exclaimed as I slid

into my seat. His eyes were bloodshot, too, but if he'd been up all night, he sure looked a whole lot better than I did.

"Thanks for the compliment," I said to him.

The other students had bleary eyes, puffy faces, and wrinkled clothes. They had been up all night like me— studying and worrying. Only Olympia appeared unaffected. She looked as if she had just come in from the Yellow Cactus Spa in Sedona after having the all-inclusive special.

Marc and I exchanged looks.

We hated her.

"How was the test?" asked Inez later that day.

"Don't ask," I told her. I had already jotted down my "I quit" speech on the back of the telephone bill envelope.

"I see," Inez replied, nodding sympathetically. "I know it will turn out," she added. "You are a smart woman, Juanita."

Not as smart as Olympia, I said to myself. I took the chores list from her and went to work. Maybe inhaling ammonia while I cleaned the bathroom would help me forget.

"Who's in?" I called over my shoulder as I headed down the hall checking off the items that I had to do.

"The Swensens have gone but Gwen already prepare the Mauve Room, is ready for the Florida couple. They'll be in tomorrow morning. Señor Williams is upstairs and Miss Hsu is in Missoula on business for your favorite person."

Speaking of my favorite person . . .

"Where is he?" I asked. I wasn't in the mood for him today. I blinked my eyes a couple of times. They were still burning from the lack of sleep. Better get some eyedrops.

Check towels, unpack new sheets, and call SW Montana
Electric . . . a few seconds passed before I realized that
Inez hadn't said anything. I turned around.

She had a funny look on her face, a combination of
confusion, thoughtfulness, and humor. In other words, her
face was screwed up in a strange way.

"Something wrong with him?"

Inez shook her head as she slipped the strap of her gigantic purse over her shoulder.

"Nada . . . pero . . ." Now, she was frowning. "Funny
thing. Señor Hayward-Smith, he eats breakfast now. I fix
him a waffle and bacon. And . . . I thought I heard him
talking to someone . . ."

"Probably Williams." My attention returned to the list
of things I had to do.

"No, Señor Williams, he was in the pantry, ironing a
shirt. I checked." Inez shrugged her shoulders as if she was
trying to throw off something. "Maybe it was the cat he
was talking to. The Siamese, he has come out of hiding."

Since Millie died, Asim had taken to hiding in the
strangest places. You would hear him howling sometimes
but you never saw him. Now that was an animal that
needed a pet shrink.

I went through the chores to keep me awake and take
my mind off of the test that I had just flunked. When I'd
finished downstairs, I headed up to the Mauve Room to
put out the "welcome" package for the Florida guests and
check the bathrooms again. Elva Van Roan had been good
but you never knew when she'd get a bug up her butt and
lock herself in.

I met Mr. High-Up Butt in the hall near the third-floor
landing. He had kind of appeared out of nowhere. I

shrieked. The house was as quiet as a tomb. For such a large man, he moved like a . . . well, like a ghost.

"Oh! Excuse me, Mrs. Louis! I'm so sorry," he said politely. "I didn't mean to startle you."

I swallowed my heart and tried to pat my hair down where it was standing straight up.

"Oh, that's OK," I said, trying to sound as if he hadn't scared my intestines clean. "I, um, can I help you with something?"

"Yes, please. I was wondering . . . well, I know how busy you are, but, if you have some time, could I have a word, Mrs. Louis?"

Please . . . I'm so sorry . . . if you have some time, I stared at Hayward-Smith. The stiffly starched white shirt had been replaced by a neat blue one, no tie. The pin-striped suit was gone; he wore khaki slacks and brown shoes. He didn't look like the hoity-toity tight ass that I had been sparring with for weeks. He didn't sound like him either. And there was something else.

Asim, the Siamese, was nestled in his arms, purring loudly, blinking his large, azure-colored eyes at me. I couldn't remember Hayward-Smith doing more than shooing the cats away before, not cuddling them.

Hayward-Smith took my silence for a "no."

"You're busy, perhaps another time . . ."

"Now is all right. More special requests, Mr. Hayward-Smith?" I asked. In my experience, when this man stooped low enough on the social scale to speak to me, he usually wanted something, like more toilet paper or another doily on the chair in his suite. "And I have two more days on that proposal." I thought I'd better remind him in case he was trying to rush me.

Hayward-Smith's cheeks reddened and he smiled slightly.

"Yes, my . . . proposal. No, Mrs. Louis, I just wanted to talk with you about something. If you have a moment."

Well, this was new: politeness, a slight stammer. Maybe he wasn't feeling well. We headed down to the back parlor. I'd left my notebook there on Millie's desk and figured that I would need it. Just inside the doorway, I stopped and stared. Millie's portrait was presiding over the room once again.

"What can I do for you, Mr. Hayward-Smith?" I asked him. Polite or not, I wasn't dropping my guard. Asim continued to purr.

"Well, you see . . . ," he cleared his throat nervously. "I want you to know that I have dropped my petition to break Mrs. Daniels's will. I have instructed my solicitors to file the appropriate documents but they have notified Mr. Black. However, I wanted to tell you . . . personally, since it was your efforts that . . . encouraged me to do it. Your inheritance is free from any interference from me, Mrs. Louis. My mother knew what she was doing when she left the inn to you. However, if you decide to sell it, I hope that you will give me the right of first refusal. And I will honor my original offer to you. I have put that in writing to Mr. Black."

You could have knocked me over with a feather. OK, maybe with a passel of feathers, not just one.

"Dropped it? You . . . wh-what did I do? Uh, you dropped it?" Yep. I made a lot of sense.

I was so relieved and surprised that I plopped down onto the red velvet settee. It had always been Millie's favorite perch. Hayward-Smith took the chair across from me, scooping up Louis and cuddling him. Cuddling. That was something else that I didn't associate with this man. What was going on?

"I don't understand."

Louis yawned and went back to sleep. He stops his naps for no one. Asim gave me a long, deep blue-eyed stare, then closed his eyes. Hayward-Smith smiled.

Smiled.

I looked at the portrait above the fireplace.

Broderick Tilson Hayward-Smith looked just like his mother.

"Don't you?" he asked. "You *are* the woman who threw a handful of papers into my face? A file folder that included a story written by . . . my mother?"

It was the very first time I had ever heard him use those words.

I felt my cheeks getting hot.

"Oh. Well, I was having a bad day . . ."

"It was a good day for me," Hayward-Smith commented. "I read that story. I read it over and over. And when I finished it, I called my solicitors. I knew that my efforts to take revenge on . . . her estate were baseless and stupid. And mean." His dark-blue eyes were steady and serious. Then Hayward-Smith was silent for a minute before he continued.

"Isn't it amazing how much we carry with us from our childhoods? We pack these slights away, both big and small, and carry them around long after we have gained the wisdom and knowledge to put them in their proper perspective."

He was asking me a question but I got the impression that he didn't want me to answer him. I looked at him and nodded. Something else about this man had now struck me. Strange as it seemed, he even *sounded* like his mother.

"You see, I was raised by David Hayward-Smith. A great statesman. A financier, philanthropist, and pillar of London society. And one of the biggest bastards who ever lived. Please excuse my language, Mrs. Louis. He never loved me. He didn't care about me at all. He only wanted me because I was a son. Had I been a daughter, I would have been thrown onto a scrap heap. I was a trophy for him just like the stuffed rhino and antelope heads he collected from his safaris. He turned me over to nannies and governesses and then packed me off to boarding school when I was eight."

Inside, I cringed at the thought of such a little boy being sent away from home.

"He allowed me to come home for the holidays. If you can call it a home. His London town house was exquisitely and expensively decorated and as cold and empty a place as you can imagine. My father was cruel and manipulative. It was only when I was grown that he allowed me the privilege of being in his presence for longer than fifteen minutes at a time. And that was only because I could be useful to him, manage his business interests so that he could retire and become a country gentleman. But by then, I hated him. And . . ."

Hayward-Smith paused and looked down at the cats that were snoozing in his lap. Then he looked up at Millie's portrait.

"And I hated her, too. For leaving me with such a man. For abandoning me to a life with this unfeeling person who never showed me a day of love or affection. I knew nothing about her and by the time I was grown, I didn't care anymore. My father had managed to poison my mind against her." He gave me a rueful smile. "So, now you have a case for a talk show. Man raised by cold, unfeeling father, abandoned by free-spirited mother."

"She didn't want to leave you!" I exclaimed.

"I know that now," Hayward-Smith replied. "Truthfully, I think I always knew it. My father married twice more and both of his wives left him. He was abusive, stingy, and mean. I knew what kind of man he was; I really couldn't blame them. I couldn't blame my mother, either. I just never knew what had happened to her. I never really even knew her real name. Father always referred to her as 'Rose.' "

I thought about the rose-bordered wallpaper in Millie's rooms. Around Paper Moon, she was Millie Tilson, the dotty old woman who lived in the big old house on the hill. But in her Paris days, she'd been "Rosie Tilson," and I remembered hearing some of the old showgirls fondly calling her "Millie Rosie" as they recounted their exploits.

"She loved you," I said, stating the obvious.

"I know she did," Hayward-Smith said, sadly. "I wish that I had known her. From what I've heard and from what I've read, she was quite a lady."

It was interesting to hear him talk about his mother that way, to hear *anyone* talk about Millie that way. I'd heard folks say "she was quite a gal." Her friends had called her a "great old broad" in their testimonials at the funeral. Everyone thought highly of Millie, even those who thought she had a screw loose. But I had never really heard anyone say that she was "quite a lady." She would have been thrilled to hear those words from her only child.

"Yes, she was," I agreed.

"I know that I haven't been the easiest guest that you've had," he commented. Yes, when he smiled, he looked just like his mother. "I would like to make it up to you. You'll have your hands full these next few months with running the inn and going to school. I put myself and my staff at your disposal. Just tell Amy what you'll need." He looked around the room for a moment. "It is important to me to keep this place going. As a tribute to my mother."

"Thank-you, Mr. Hayward-Smith," I told him. Now, all I had to figure out was what the hell I was going to do with it!

"Just 'Rick,'" he said simply. "I actually prefer to be called Rick." Then he got an impish expression on his face. It looked so out of character that I almost laughed. He looked just like Millie had when she was about to do something mischievous. "Unless you want to keep calling me 'Mr. Pointy-Nose High-Up Butt' I can answer to that name, too."

"No, no, Rick will be fine," I said quickly. When had he heard me call him those names? Now, it was my turn to feel embarrassed.

"Oh, and Mrs. Louis?"

"Juanita will be fine, thanks," I said, my cheeks still burning.

"Montana has given me quite an appetite. I'll have to watch my weight while I'm here. I would like to spend a certain number of weeks at the inn every year. And, when I'm here, do you think you could prevail upon Mr. Gardiner to include catfish and collard greens on the menu more often?" His eyes sparkled with amusement. "Oh, and extra rolls next time, if you don't mind, Mrs. Louis." He added in the stiff cadence that only Hayward-Smith could use. "I didn't have enough to sop up the gravy with."

"I don't know what you did or how you did it," commented Geoff Black, the attorney for Millie's estate, "but Mr. Hayward-Smith is being very, very generous."

Not only had Rick dropped the will contest but he had also supplemented the annuity that his mother left to keep up the old house. It was over one hundred years old and there was always something going wrong. Right now, it needed roof repair, a new air-conditioning unit for the top floors and new sidewalks. Rick's ideas were like Millie's— practical and creative at the same time. Later, when I told him that he reminded me of his mother, he blushed.

"You don't know what it means to hear you say that," he told me. He looked so happy, so different from the man who I had made fun of by calling him names. I kinda felt bad about that. "Funny thing, though . . ."

"Yes?" I said.

"Elva Van Roan said the very same thing, just the other day," he said thoughtfully.

I almost fell through the floor. *He* was talking to Elva. As far as I knew, the only person around this house who had ever had a conversation with Elva was Millie. I didn't count myself, of course.

I could have sworn that Millie winked at me from the portrait over the fireplace.

Wednesday's class was out of control. Because of the Memorial Day holiday, we'd had a long weekend, which was both good and bad. Good to have the time off, Jess and I had spent it visiting his relatives in Boise, bad because it stretched out the time before we got our grades on the test. Chef sauntered into the classroom as he always did, always on time yet never appearing to be in a hurry. He greeted us all and reached into the black leather portfolio that he carried his class notes in. Like second-graders, we got real quiet now that the teacher was here.

"Ladies, gentlemen," Chef greeted us in his usual continental way. "I am very pleased to return your examinations. I must say that I was surprised at the results but I think I can safely say that this group has promise. Some of you will have done much better than you thought, some of you did as you expected, and others of you will be disappointed." He looked around the room as he said this. Olympia flipped her hair over her shoulders (it's a wonder she didn't snap her neck doing that) and straightened her body a little when Chef's glance fell on her.

I sighed. Marc, who sat next to me, was antsy. He was drumming his fingers on the desk and bouncing his knee up and down. The tapping and the smacking of his sneakered foot on the floor were more than I could take in my state of nerves.

"Will you quit it?" I whispered loudly, glaring at him. I have adopted Marc. He reminds me of Randy and Rashawn rolled up into one. He has Rashawn's focus and tenacity (unfortunately, of course, Rashawn is using his focus on illicit drug sales) and Randy's playfulness and sense of humor. And he's hyper. Randy could never sit still for a minute.

"Sorry," he said.

Chef handed Marc his paper and moved on to me. I held my breath. I didn't want to look at it. Chef said, "Hard work and persistence always pay off, Madame Louis."

B-plus.

I got a *B-plus*!!!!

"Good shit!" Marc exclaimed, looking over my shoulder. "You've been holding out on me! You've got this stuff down cold!"

He had squeaked by with a C-plus but he was grateful for that. I glanced around the class. Some of the other students were grinning, some were not. And, which was very interesting, Olympia looked as if she was about to cry. I found out later that she'd gotten a D. I was stunned.

Marc was not surprised, though.

"High expectations, low preparations, mediocre results," he said, using uncharacteristically scholarly words.

"Where did you get that pearl of wisdom?" I asked him as we moved into our teams to tackle petits fours.

"My father," he said glumly. "He was always telling us shit like that when we were growing up."

"Sounds as if your father is a very wise man," I told him. We both found out later that Marc was right—Olympia hadn't studied as much as the rest of us because advanced mathematics was her forte and she felt confident that she would do well. Marc and I had studied our butts off. Our confidence had only extended as far as putting the right name on the paper. Beyond that, we had just said a prayer and hoped that we had done enough.

I guess we had.

"Don't swish the cake around in the fondant," Chef instructed, the Irish lilt in his voice rising as he belted out the message. "Just give it a good dip, turn it slightly, and let the mixture drip down the sides. Good, Alisa."

Marc's first effort barely had any of the sticky white icing on it at all. His second was at the opposite end of the spectrum; there was fondant dripping down the fork. Dipping petits fours is a two-handed operation, not one of my strong points. So I watched Marc for a few moments then took a deep breath and moved to try a few myself. Just as I grabbed the fork, I heard Chef's voice from behind me.

"Ah, Juanita. Let's see them."

I sighed. Speared the little square one, said a quick prayer, and held it over the creamy white icing. As I dunked it in, it promptly slid off the fork. Oh, no! For half a second, I didn't know what to do! But, just as the bottom half of the cake started to disappear into the quicksand-like icing, I stabbed at the little cake cube, speared it, and rescued it from the quagmire. Marc and some of my class-mates applauded.

"Good save," Marc said with admiration.

Chef cleared his throat.

"You'll get the hang of it sooner or later," he said, not commenting on my miraculous rescue.

I decided that I had done something marvelous. Let's face it, you haven't lived until you've dropped a petit four into a bowl of fondant and recovered it, one-handed, using a plastic fork.

Chapter Fifteen

Montana finally shrugged off winter and plunged right into a summer for the weather record books: hot and dry one minute, hot and steamy the next. For the first time in twenty years, there were forest fires north of Paper Moon near Glacier. It got pretty scary. The rains were very slow in coming. And when they did come, the moisture they brought wasn't enough to put out a Girl Scout campfire. I could smell the dark, peatlike aroma of the burning trees when I stood on the porch of the diner in the morning. Some days, the air was light and sweet like a spicy French perfume—woodsy, dark, full of amber, and trimmed with smoke. On the other mornings, the burning timber smoke was thick and persistent. It glued itself to my lungs and made me cough. It stung my eyes. Sometimes I wondered if Montana would burn up and blow away on a future breeze. It didn't. The fires eventually burned themselves out. Montana remained.

The fires painted the early evening skies of late summer

the colors of fresh peach and strawberry ice cream but we knew that the beauty was dangerous and false. Arcadia Lake rose and fell like a yo-yo. I watered my geraniums first thing in the morning and last thing before sundown. Many days, it was too hot to be outside at all. At dusk, it cooled down, but you had to box with mosquitoes the size of hummingbirds. They had the flying expertise of World War II pilots swooping down out of the sky, making a perfect landing on an uncovered arm or neck. You needed a baseball bat to swat at them. There were a lot of days when the weather felt more like Paper Moon, Arizona, than it did Paper Moon, Montana. And, as people always do, we complained about the weather. We'd whined when the snowdrifts were up to our butts. Now we whined again because the thermometer was stuck at ninety degrees and we daydreamed of cooler days.

August came and, as the calendar moved into double digits, the evening temperatures began to drop, half a degree at a time, hardly noticeable at first, except at night. Sometimes, I thought I smelled frost on the evening air, just a hint of ice. A whisper to us that fall was on its way, that seasons change and nothing stays the same.

Peaches's Purple Passion roared into the parking lot of the diner one late-August afternoon. I hadn't seen Peaches in three months but we'd traded e-mails. Well, she had, anyway. I'm better at pressing "delete" than "enter," a problem if you've deleted the message you are supposed to reply *to*.

Dracula barked to let us know that we had another customer then went back to his nap. The rig stirred up a lot of gravel and dust but its wax job was still in place. The truck finally settled itself into its city block–sized parking space and the engine idled down. I heard a door slam. Stacy walked around the front of the truck cab, waving.

"There's Stacy!" I exclaimed, heading for the door. It had been awhile since I'd seen her—Stacy usually drives the eastern routes. I liked Stacy—she was as gregarious as Peaches and just as hardworking. When she drove, she liked to listen to Stephen King thrillers and opera. *The Shining* and *The Magic Flute* were her favorites. She said that the horror stories sometimes scared her so much that she was afraid to get out of the truck!

"Juanita, you're a sight for sore eyes!" Stacy said, giving me a warm hug. Tall and slim where Peaches was shorter and stockier, Stacy has short, dark curly hair and green eyes.

"It's good to see you and good to see this place." Stacy rubbed her hands together. Stacy only looked like a toothpick—this was a woman who could throw down some food. "What does Jess have good to eat?"

"Yeah, what're the specials? I'm starving half to death!" Peaches yelled from the cab. She had her elbow on the windowsill and was grinning like a fool. "I hope you have some grub, Miss Juanita. None of that highbrow stuff you're learning about in coolin' airey school."

I held my hand up to my forehead to block the late-afternoon sun.

"We might have a crumb or two. Are you going to come down from your throne, Your Highness?" I shouted up at her. " 'Cause if you think we have curb service, you are going to be disappointed."

"I need to report y'all to the Better Business Bureau," Peaches commented, shaking her head in mock dismay. "Surly cook and no curbside service. What's happening to this country? Not at all like the good old days."

I laughed. Peaches is so silly. And then I stopped laughing. Stacy had swung the purple door open and was now helping a *very* pregnant Peaches maneuver down the steps. My mouth dropped open.

"Well, this is a fine thing," Peaches said loudly to Stacy, using a sarcastic tone. She grunted a little as she slowly put one foot then the other down on the ground. "You would think she'd never seen a pregnant woman before. It isn't polite to stare, Juanita." Her eyes sparkled. Beside her, Stacy smiled proudly.

I don't think I had ever seen a belly so *big!*

"How did this happen?" I asked, and then shut my mouth. I gave her a hug. Well, I tried to give her a hug. I ended up hugging her from the side because her belly was in the way!

Peaches gave me a sideways look.

"OK . . . but I thought that . . ." I looked at Stacy. She grinned and started rubbing Peaches's back.

They had talked about Stacy having a baby last year but I didn't hear anything more about it for a long time. So I just forgot about the whole thing. Then I remembered Arizona and Peaches's visit to Nina, her giving up cigarettes and beer, all of a sudden, and the fact that she'd looked under the weather for several months in the spring. Not to mention that her appetite had fallen off. The day Peaches eats a piece of toast and ginger ale? I should have known then but, with all of the bugs and viruses going around, I just thought she was having a hard time getting over that flu.

Peaches shrugged as we moved toward the diner. Stacy and I walked, Peaches waddled.

"We had some tests done. Stacy had some issues."

Peaches sighed and stretched a little. "I didn't have any issues sooooo . . ." She gave her belly a gentle pat. "Here we
are! All of us!"

"Lord, yes," I said. Together Stacy and I helped Peaches
up the steps. "And should you be gallivanting around the
countryside in that truck?"

Both women laughed.

"This is her last trip, doctor's orders," Stacy answered.
"The baby is due in early November but they don't think
she'll make it until then."

"I don't think I'll make it until tonight," Peaches groaned.
"I feel as if I'm carrying around the Superdome."

"Baby?" I looked at the Mount Everest–sized mound
around Peaches's middle. "Are you sure that there is only
one in there?"

Peaches chuckled.

"Some days it feels like a rugby team, fighting and
wrestling. But the ultrasound shows one child. The little
twerp rolled up into a ball so we can't tell whether it will
be a girl or a boy."

Jess had opened the door for us and shook his head
when he saw Peaches.

"Guess we'll have to open a day care center," he commented. He had Teishia in his arms. They were both eating Popsicles and had sticky faces.

"You see what I have to deal with." I sighed. *Where was
that pack of Wet Ones?*

"How do you feel about being a godmother?" Peaches
asked.

"Oh, I think I can squeeze you in," I said, giving her
another sideways hug. "Somewhere between the puffed
pastry and petits fours, Millie's bed-and-breakfast, and Big

Bird." *Business, Math II, Menu planning, Labor Day, my Spanish lessons . . . and a trip to Mexico.*

Once upon a time, I had a COTA bus life. I got up, ate the same kind of cereal, smoked the same brand of cigarettes, and got on the same bus every day, going to the same job. I thought the same thoughts and figured that, if I lived long enough, I might have thirty more years or so of the same thing: bus passes, empty Coke bottles, a blaring TV, fried chicken, and church twice on Sundays and once on Wednesday nights to eat up the long empty moments when I got old. It was a safe enough life, if you could call it a life. Without hopes or dreams, you don't have much to look forward to. I didn't allow myself to hope. Dreams were something that other people had.

Fat chance of that happening to me now. I have so many hairpin turns, sudden starts and stops, that it is a wonder that I don't have whiplash. And I don't have any more answers about the secret of life than I did when I started. If anything, I have more questions.

The inn is booked every week until it closes in October and I'm busier than a sand flea on a beach. For the first time in my life, I am a businesswoman.

Millie's son, Rick, has been as good as his word, better, actually. The old house got a face-lift as soon as the weather broke: roof, air-conditioning, sidewalks, paint, everything. A very fancy and very expensive magazine ad has kept the phones ringing. And I am going to write a cookbook. I already have the title: *Juanita's Put-Your-Foot-In-It Cookbook.*

Randy is spending his vacation in Montana. He and Jess are "refining" the dinner menus at the diner. They are quite a pair.

"Just don't get too fancy," I have warned them. "A slice

of blood-rare meat and a sprig of parsley do not a decent meal make. Especially in this country."

They ignore me, but as I walk away, I hear Jess ask Randy, "What does 'suddity' mean?"

Teishia is staying with us for a while and she is a joy. Randy brought her with him for a visit. She starts Saint Dominic's Pre-School in September. I guess Bertie was listening to some of the things I said.

There are no heartwarming endings there. Bertie has come a long way: She has a new job making almost twice what she did at Kroger's. She has a new apartment and gets "A"s in the business courses that she takes. Randy knows her boyfriend, Victor. Says that he is a gentle, hardworking man who is good to my daughter and good to Teishia.

But Bertie and I don't have cozy mother-daughter chats. I wish we did. We don't call each other to chitchat about something we saw on the TV. She does not ask me for advice. When I said good-bye to Bertie last winter, we did not hug. I see Mary and Mignon together and I wish that things could be different. But wishing is not enough.

Rashawn is still a businessman—the demand for his products has yet to dry up. He is coldly polite when we talk on the phone, which is hardly ever. No sunshine and blue skies there, either.

I graduate next year in May. I will have an associate's degree. It's not a PhD but it is a start. Chefs are a hot commodity. I have received offers from resorts, spas (including the Yellow Cactus because Nina refuses to give up on me), hotels, and luxury cruise lines. Next spring, I become a woman with credentials. I will have to decide what to do with them.

"The Ritz-Carlton? Humph. That sounds suddity, if you ask me," Jess said, smugly.

My mother said that I was a slow learner. It took me
nearly forty years to figure out that she was right. I have
been living life backward, picking up pieces and parts of
the lessons of living in the afternoon of my life, lessons
that other folks learned in morning kindergarten. My head
got real hard from the knocks, bumps, and bruises. And
my soul had no protection, because I had forgotten that I
had a soul until it was hardly there at all, just a small puff
of smoke left over from a match struck two minutes
ago, the rumor of a memory. Just before it was too late, I
reached out with both hands, grabbed at my soul, and
pulled it back before it slipped away and left me forever.
Souls don't stick around to see if you're going to grow into
them or not. They have better things to do.

I'm starting over now, going off to taste and see what I
missed. Some of my destinations are new and unfamiliar;
others are roads worn down by my footsteps but now I
walk them wearing a different pair of shoes. Not all of my
trips are journeys of the foot. More often now, I am a voy-
ager of the spirit, and those are the journeys that can hurt
the most but bring the most joy.

I move, slowly and with aching joints, but I move, even
if I don't know exactly where I'm going. I know that I will
be OK. I have found my place in this world. And it has
nothing to do with geography. A fish doesn't drown in
water and birds don't fall out of the air. Every creature that
God makes flies best when it flies in its own way and in its
own space. And I have found mine.

Jess and I don't talk about the future. We take each
morning as it comes, we work hard, we love hard, and we
get on with life. There is a fork coming in the road in a few
months—for both of us. I might be cruising in the Medi-

terranean next year this time or I might be flipping crepes for spa guests in Sonoma Valley, or baking pecan brownies for the Eagle Scouts in Mason, and popping toast for breakfast guests at Millie's place. Lately, Jess has talked about selling the diner and retiring. To go into business with *me*.

I still read when I have the time. But I have noticed something about the endings of my books. Maybe it was there all the time and I wasn't ready to see it. At the end of a romance novel, the money is in the bank, the villain has been locked up forever, and the heroine has her man. Love triumphant. The endings of the sci-fi sagas are not as sugary—the villain is lost in space somewhere but he, she, or it will be back in the sequel. In the meantime, though, the two suns are shining, the galaxy is safe, and there is, finally, enough food and water to feed the colony for a while until they can figure out what to do next. In the westerns, the cattle can graze, the coyote are dead, and the water rights have been protected. And in highbrow literature, the protagonist or the antagonist (it depends on your point of view) is either ready to commit suicide or close the draperies and sit in the dark, enlightened and alone but not lonely.

This is fiction. Real life falls somewhere between "they lived happily ever after" and "life is hell and then you die." So you dance along the edge of a tin roof and the rain soaks you and you dodge the lightning bolts and you slip once or twice in your high heels and, sometimes, you almost fall off. But if you don't, you'll see a rainbow and it will have been worth it.

I didn't find a new life in Paper Moon, Montana. I made myself one. That wise woman who said that there are years that ask you questions and there are years that answer left out something. There are years that answer with more questions.

Rick still offers to buy Millie's place. He says that it has become his second home.

"Same terms, same price. Whenever you're ready."

I think about it once in a while. It's an offer that allows me to keep some windows open, to let impossible possibilities inside. The beat-up blue suitcase sits patiently in the back of the closet. Waiting . . .

I look out across the highway at the cool, dark-green forests of Kaylin's Ridge. I watch the dancing raindrops on Arcadia Lake. And, beyond the forests, I remember the plains and the snow-capped Rockies and the skies that go on forever. And the summer storms that Idaho sends eastward with their lightning and thunder and rains. I treasure the way Paper Moon makes me feel. This is Juanita's place, the home that I will always carry with me in my heart.

On the Right Side
of a Dream

A Reader's Guide

Sheila Williams

Reading Group Questions and
Topics for Discussion

Reader's Guide questions developed by Patricia Hooks Gray. Ms. Gray is a graduate of Fisk University, Nashville, Tennessee, and Xavier University, Cincinnati, Ohio. She taught in the Princeton, Ohio, school system and is an adjunct professor at Xavier University, where she teaches graduate- and undergraduate-level reading courses. Ms. Gray also writes units for the Core Knowledge Foundation on subjects involving reading and social studies.

1. How did fear, anger, and quiet shame nearly suffocate Juanita's soul? What actions did she take to create an emotional balance?

2. Why can't Juanita and Bertie get past their differences? What advice would you give them?

3. Take stock of Juanita's life. Explain how her failures paved the way to her success and eventual happiness.

4. Do you think Peaches and Stacy have set their souls free? Were they on the right or the wrong side of their dream?

5. Colors permeated the novel and offered vivid imagery for the reader. What colors represented the different stages of Juanita's personal development through the story?

6. How did Juanita devalue her sense of self? When did the cycle of low self-esteem break for her?

7. Would you consider Millie a modern "Renaissance" woman? If so, why?

8. Millie turned out to be a mentor for Juanita. What lessons did Juanita learn from Millie that affected her life?

9. As Juanita made changes in her life, how did she gain a sense of serenity and control? Some of her dreams turned into reality. How did she spread her "wings" and fly?

10. How did Juanita's growth enhance her children's lives? What is likely to happen to Rashawn?

11. Money was dangled in front of Millie and Juanita. Discuss how the decisions they made concerning money affected their lives.

12. "Money is at the root of all evil." Should Millie have taken her child? Was it more about the money, herself, or the baby?

13. Did Hayward-Smith have every right to feel the way he did about his mother? How were love and forgiveness key in his feelings for her?

14. Jess was a rare jewel. How had Juanita found real love in him? How was he her soul mate?

15. Share how the novel exposes the internal hurts of the characters that gnawed away large bits of their hearts.

16. If you could create your ideal life, what would *you* dare to dream?

ABOUT THE AUTHOR

SHEILA WILLIAMS was born in Columbus, Ohio. She attended Ohio Wesleyan University and is a graduate of the University of Louisville in Louisville, Kentucky. She and her husband have two grown children and make their home in northern Kentucky.

ABOUT THE TYPE

This book was set in Weiss, a typeface designed by a German artist, Emil Rudolf Weiss (1875–1942). The designs of the roman and italic were completed in 1928 and 1931 respectively. The Weiss types are rich, well-balanced, and even in color, and they reflect the subtle skill of a fine calligrapher.